"What are you doing in here, Belle?"

"Sorry, Brady, but the bedside light was on and I came in to switch it off for you." The explanation sounded lame even to Isabella's ears.

"In that case I'd say you have a very weak excuse for coming into my bedroom," he drawled lazily, but the grim tone had disappeared now, replaced by one of amusement. "Was there any other reason for you coming in here?"

"What other reason could I possibly have?" The question and the hand holding her made her tremble inside.

"I don't know of any except the age-old one..." he drawled sardonically.

KATHRYN ROSS was born in Zambia, where her parents happened to live at the time. Educated in Ireland and England, she now lives in a village near Blackpool, Lancashire. Kathryn is a professional beauty therapist, but writing is her first love. As a child she wrote adventure stories, and at thirteen she was editor of her school magazine. Happily, ten writing years later *Designed with Love* was accepted by Harlequin. A romantic Sagittarian, she loves traveling to exotic locations.

Scent of Betrayal

KATHRYN ROSS

SWEET REVENGE

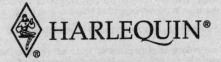

HARLEQUIN®

TORONTO • NEW YORK • LONDON
AMSTERDAM • PARIS • SYDNEY • HAMBURG
STOCKHOLM • ATHENS • TOKYO • MILAN • MADRID
PRAGUE • WARSAW • BUDAPEST • AUCKLAND

ISBN 0-373-80549-7

SCENT OF BETRAYAL

First North American Publication 2001.

CHAPTER ONE

How could a passion so deep, so all-consuming, turn to such hatred? Isabella found herself wondering as she met Brady Webster's eyes briefly across the boardroom table. She took a deep breath and looked away before launching into the attack.

She was the only female seated at the long, polished table and, to make matters worse, at twenty-six years of age she was by far the youngest member of the board. She could feel the resentment of the men seated around that table; it hung in the air, almost like a tangible force, ready to envelop her and stifle her if she made one wrong move.

'So, gentlemen, if you would like to turn to my proposals on page seven...' Her voice was clear and steady, yet inside she quivered with nerves. The rustle of turning pages broke the silence for a moment, then there was a deep hush as eyes moved over the printed page.

'These proposals are outrageous.' Richard Fox was the first to speak, his tone extremely angry. 'I don't know what your father would make of such utter nonsense.'

'I can assure you that Tom read my report before he went into hospital, Richard, and he approved of my ideas.' Isabella spoke calmly. She was surprised that Richard was the first to object to these new ideas.

Richard had worked alongside her father for many years at Brook Mollinar and had become a shareholder at the company fifteen years ago. She had thought that he at least would give her a fair chance, yet his face held a closed, angry expression. Isabella felt sure he hadn't even thought about the ideas in front of him. Maybe, like a lot of people around this table, he resented the intrusion of a young woman and he was embittered by the fact that Isabella's father had transferred all of his shares over to her, placing her in an extremely powerful position.

'Exactly which aspect of my ideas do you not like?' she asked now in a polite tone.

The older man's eyes flicked in a tired way down towards the paper in front of him. 'This green issue, for one.' He practically spat the words out. 'Brook Mollinar is a cosmetics house with style. The women who buy our perfume do so because we have the reputation for quality. When they take out the distinctive glass bottle of "Destiny" and spray it on it speaks of opulence, of money being no object, of utter luxury. It should not speak of economy, of green issues.'

'Why not?' Isabella batted the question back at him crisply. 'Surely the whole world should be concerned with the green issue. As for economy, the world is also concerned with that issue. It may have escaped your notice, Richard, but a lot of countries are going through recession at the moment, which is partly the reason why our sales are down.'

The men started talking between themselves and Isabella took the opportunity to sort through her papers to find the latest sales figures. Her head was bent, but she was conscious of Brady's dark eyes watching her. He was chairing the meeting, yet apart from clipped commands he had said very little. It was an ominous silence.

What was he thinking? she wondered nervously. Was he thinking how much she had changed since he had last seen her eight years ago? Or was he thinking purely of business? Stupid question; Brady would of course be calculating out the figures she had placed before him. Brady had a brilliant mind—a mind like a computer, Tom had always said. That was part of the reason he had taken him on as director ten years ago.

She looked up and her eyes clashed with his again. The impact made a jolt of shivers race down her spine and she averted her gaze quickly. One thing was sure: Brady hadn't changed much over the years; he was still extremely attractive. He still had a most peculiar effect on her pulse-rate.

'Sales are down by nearly twenty per cent,' she forced herself to carry on briskly. 'That's a hell of a drop since the start of the year.'

Nobody argued that point.

'So I take it you are going to solve all our problems with phials of perfume to refill the glass atomisers?' Richard asked scornfully.

Isabella felt a surge of irritation. Did he have to be so negative, and didn't anyone else have anything to say? 'I think it will help,' she answered without prevarication. 'Our glass atomisers are very beautiful and also very expensive to produce. If we offer refills for them we will be cutting cost production for ourselves and we will be able to pass on that saving to our customers; they will no longer have to throw their bottle away, therefore we have a greener product.'

'You do realise that the design for the bottle will have to be changed so that they can accommodate a refill tube?' Richard asked crossly.

'Yes, if you turn to the next page you will see that I have prepared a cost analysis.' Isabella watched as everyone turned the pages—everyone, that was, except Brady. He had already read the report from cover to cover while Richard had been talking.

She glanced surreptitiously over at him. He was glancing at the gold Swiss watch on his wrist, a look of irritation on his lean features.

The thick dark hair was tinged with silver now, Isabella noticed idly, but nothing else had changed. He wore a stylish grey suit that seemed to emphasise the superbly fit body, and a white shirt that contrasted with a lightly tanned skin. At thirty-seven, Brady Webster was even more attractive than he had been eight years ago.

He looked over at her, a gleam of amusement in the arrogant darkness of his eyes. He knew she had been studying him. Irritation flared inside her. Why was she so damn curious about Brady? She knew what he was; she had learnt the lesson well a long time ago.

'I never realised that you were an environmentalist, Belle,' he murmured smoothly. It was the first time he had spoken directly to her since he had entered the room, and for some reason the deep velvet voice disturbed her intensely.

'I care about the issues that are important.' She was instantly on the defensive; she would not allow Brady to poke fun at her. She wasn't about to give this man an inch.

He nodded his head. 'I like your ideas.'

'You do?' The words just slipped out. She had been preparing herself for an almighty confrontation with Brady. He was the one person who she had been certain she would clash with, but instead the enemy seemed almost congenial.

'I think, gentlemen, that Isabella has some sound ideas.' He spoke in a louder, more commanding tone down the long table. 'Brook Mollinar has always prided itself on being a caring company; for example, we do not test any of our products on animals. Therefore should it also not follow that we concern ourselves with caring for the environment?'

There was a low mumble of approval, but Brady didn't

give anyone a chance to interrupt before he pushed the point home. 'We can launch the new atomisers with a big advertising campaign. Brook Mollinar will be shown as the company that not only cares about the way you look and feel, but also the world around you. We will be seen to be "green" and meanwhile sales will rise.'

Everyone now seemed to be in favour of the idea, Isabella noticed with some rancour. Strange how they had disliked the idea five minutes ago when she had voiced it, but when backed by Brady it was suddenly most acceptable.

She turned sparkling, angry blue eyes on to him. 'I am not saying that we should be "seen to be green",' she told him crisply. 'I'm saying that we should be green.'

'I know what you're saying.' He was busy making notes and he didn't bother to look up at her. His tone was one that would be used to pacify an irritating child. Then he swept on briskly. 'Now, gentlemen, I suggest we put Isabella's proposal to the vote.'

The proposal was voted through with a speed that made Isabella dizzy, then the other items on the agenda were dealt with in an equally brisk and efficient manner. Brady was obviously in a hurry and wasn't about to wait around for anyone.

'I think that brings us to the tenth item on our list—our new perfume. As yet we have no name for it, but Claude at our factory in the South of France has assured me that it is on schedule for the autumn.' Brady paused and looked down the long table. 'As you know, a lot of money has gone into the research of this perfume. Claude assures me that his results are very exciting indeed. I suggest we call a separate meeting to discuss the perfume exclusively when I come back from seeing him next week.'

'You're seeing Claude next week?' She didn't mean her voice to sound so sharp.

'That's right. I fly back to Nice day after tomorrow. I'll see him after the weekend.' Dark eyes met her directly. 'Is there some problem?'

She hesitated. There was a problem, a very big one. It was the very thing that she had come in prepared to face. Yet suddenly she was changing her mind. 'No...no problem.' She backed down. This morning had shown her one thing very clearly. The men around this table did not trust her yet, but they did trust Brady Webster. She couldn't voice her suspicions yet.

'Then I think we should adjourn the meeting and schedule another for the week after next.' Brady was starting to close his files.

Isabella watched as he started to put them in his briefcase. She had to say something. 'Before we close, there is a question I would like to ask.'

'Yes?' He stopped what he was doing and looked over at her.

'As everyone here knows, you are also managing director of the Swiss pharmaceuticals company Wolf-Chem. I believe that they are branching out into cosmetics?'

He nodded. 'Yes, that is correct.' His manner was matter-of-fact, his dark eyes watchful.

'Don't you think that move presents you with a serious conflict of interests?' Isabella asked swiftly.

'No, I don't. Do you?'

Isabella didn't know what reaction she had expected from him, but it certainly wasn't this blatant manner of throwing the question back at her. 'Well, yes, I do. I think it presents all kinds of problems. You are in effect managing director of what is now a rival company.'

'Wolf-Chem are only going into cosmetics in a small way; I don't think they will present any serious competition,' Brady informed her crisply. 'But, even if they were, I have a vested interest in both companies, so I want to see both do well. It doesn't present any problems for Brook Mollinar.' He glanced down the table. 'Does anyone think it will?'

There was a general shaking of heads. 'Certainly not.' Richard spoke for everyone.

'Good.' Brady looked directly at her again. 'Does that answer your question?' he asked calmly.

Isabella nodded. It certainly did answer it. It told her quite clearly that the members of the board trusted Brady Webster implicitly. But she didn't, she thought with an inward tremor. She didn't trust the man an inch.

The meeting came to a close. Richard came over to speak to her before leaving. 'How's your father?'

'A lot better than he was. I'm hoping they're going to allow him out of hospital at the weekend.'

'Good. Give him my regards.'

'I will, thank you, Richard.' Out of the corner of her eye she could see Brady putting on his overcoat. She had forgotten just how tall he was.

'Perhaps I'll call up to the house to see him next week.'

Richard had her full attention now. She sincerely hoped that if he called to see her father he didn't start worrying him with the business. Tom had been told to avoid any kind of stress after this, his second heart attack, and he had been allowed no visitors except for family at the hospital. 'That would be nice, Richard. If you do, I would appreciate it if you keep the conversation light.'

'What Belle is saying, Richard, is don't place any unnecessary worries about the business into Tom's mind,' Brady interjected bluntly from beside them.

Isabella glared over at him. 'I was just trying to explain that Tom has to take things easy now.'

'That's all right, Isabella, I do understand,' Richard said smoothly. Then he patted her shoulder in a fatherly way.

'By the way, welcome to the board. I don't believe anyone
said that to you today.'

'Thanks, Richard.' She watched him go and then, suddenly realising that she was now alone in the room with
Brady, she reached nervously for her coat.

She could feel his eyes moving over her slender figure.
She was wearing a red Chanel suit that was elegant yet
businesslike. The skirt stopped just above the knee, showing a glimpse of long, shapely legs in sheer black stock-
ings. Four years of living in Paris had changed Isabella,
groomed her into a very sophisticated woman. She felt she
was a different person from the one Brady had known so
long ago. He took everything in, from the height of her
black court shoes to the tip of her gleaming blonde hair,
which was drawn severely back from her face and secured
in a French plait.

'You are looking well, Belle.' The compliment was de-
livered in a casual tone.

'Thanks.' She wished he wouldn't shorten her name like
that; it sounded far too intimate. She struggled nervously
with her coat and he reached to hold it for her.

'Thanks,' she muttered again, pulling back sharply as
his hand brushed against her shoulder. Her eyes flickered
up to his face and caught the glimmer of amusement in
his dark eyes. Damn the man, he knew he was unnerving
her and he was enjoying every minute of it.

'Are you glad to be back in London?' he asked conversationally.

Isabella shrugged. 'For the time being.' She didn't want
to get into conversation with Brady, and her tone told him
that very clearly.

'Ah…missing your French boyfriend?' he remarked
with a slight twist of his lips.

She looked up at him sharply. What the hell did he know
about her French boyfriend? she wondered angrily. The

man had no damn right to ask such an impertinent question.

Brady saw the expression in her eyes and smiled. 'Your father keeps me informed about you. He tells me that you have plans to marry this man… What's his name? Giles?'

'Julien.' Isabella could feel her blood-pressure rising sharply.

'Well, he's certainly done things for you,' Brady remarked idly. He reached out a hand and tipped her chin up with a gentle finger so that she was forced to look directly at him. 'You no longer wear your glasses, I notice.'

The soft touch of his hand against her skin was electric. A dull flush of colour rose up under her creamy skin as he studied her face with intense interest. She pulled away from him, trembling with anger at his audacity. How dared he touch her like that?

'Either your eyesight has improved dramatically, or you are wearing contact lenses,' he continued, impervious to the frosty reception his remarks were getting.

'What on earth is this sudden interest in my appearance, Brady?' Her voice quivered with anger.

'I wouldn't say there was anything sudden about it,' he replied easily. 'I was always interested by your appearance.'

They were treading on dangerous ground now. It took all of Isabella's self-control not to say something she would later regret. She allowed the remark to pass in silence and reached to pick up her briefcase.

'How about having dinner with me tonight, Belle?'

The quietly asked question caught her by surprise and it took a few moments for her to formulate an answer. 'No, thank you, Brady, I'm busy this evening.' Why on earth was he inviting her to dinner? she wondered. She slanted a sharp look up at him. What was he up to?

'Tomorrow night, then?' he persisted.

'Busy then too. In fact I'm busy every night where you are concerned.' She started to make for the door, her head held high.

'Pity. We could do with having a talk.' He fell in step beside her out into the silent corridor towards the lifts.

'I don't think we have anything to talk about, Brady,' she said calmly.

The lift doors swished open and they both stepped in. She pressed one well manicured finger at the button for the lower floor. She was very anxious to be away from this man. The close confines of the lift were decidedly unsettling.

'On the contrary. I think we have a lot to discuss,' he murmured drily. 'We could talk about old times... You and I used to be friends.'

Friends! Somewhere deep a thrust of anger turned inside her.

'And you are now a major shareholder in Brook Mollinar,' he continued smoothly. 'I would like to talk about the direction the company is taking, plans for the future. I would especially like to discuss the new perfume with you before going to Nice at the weekend.'

'I see.' For a moment Isabella had to fight to keep her voice steady. Brady wasn't interested in talking about old times; he was more concerned about power and manipulation. She was a major shareholder and suddenly he wanted to take her to dinner...very convenient. 'As I said before, I am very busy. You will have to reserve anything you wish to say to me until the next board meeting.'

A look of irritation flashed across the strong, handsome features and he stretched out a hand to stop the lift.

'What on earth do you think you are doing?' There was a note of panic in her voice as she looked up at him.

'As this seems to be our only opportunity of having a

quiet word I thought I would take it,' he grated. 'Point number one; I have invested a lot of money and a lot of time into this company. I will not see all my efforts and hard work go down the drain because of some imagined grudge you seem to have against me.'

Imagined grudge! Brady Webster had a very convenient memory, she thought furiously. 'I don't have the faintest idea what you are talking about,' she said calmly.

'No?' One dark eyebrow lifted sardonically. 'Then suppose you tell me why you don't want to take the time to discuss these important points with me?'

'Because quite frankly, Brady, I don't feel like discussing future plans for the company with you. Especially plans for our new perfume.' She took a strange kind of pleasure in hitting out verbally at him. For a moment her temper overtook discretion.

'I see.' Dark eyes narrowed. 'Do you mind explaining why not?'

'Do I really need to spell it out to you?' she asked scornfully. 'I think I've already voiced my doubts at the meeting.' She reached across and calmly pushed the button for the ground floor again.

He frowned. 'You mean my involvement with Wolf-Chem?'

'You are managing director for a rival company, Brady. That fact in itself gives me cause for concern.'

The handsome features hardened. 'Just what are you trying to accuse me of?'

'I'm not accusing you of anything,' she cut across him firmly. 'Let's just say I have certain misgivings.'

'Misgivings about what?' he asked grimly.

The lift doors opened into the entrance lobby and Isabella stepped out thankfully. She had no wish to continue the conversation; she had already said too much.

'Misgivings about what, Isabella?' Brady's voice had an

ominous ring to it and all of the receptionists at the desk looked over at them.

'That is all I'm prepared to say, Brady,' Isabella said in a low tone. 'Now good day.'

She crossed the red carpet towards the glass doors, nodding politely to the staff as she passed them. She could feel Brady's presence behind her and her heart beat a rapid nervous tattoo in her chest. She had the awful feeling that he was going to create a scene right here in front of the staff. However, he said nothing until they were outside, and then he grabbed her quite forcibly by the elbow.

'Now explain exactly what you meant by that last statement.' It was a demand issued in a tone that was definitely not one to be ignored.

She glared up at him, her mind whirling frantically. It had been a mistake to start this. She had never meant to go so far with it. She took a deep breath and decided that the only thing she could do now was change track. 'I'm sorry, Brady,' she murmured, looking up at him with huge blue eyes. 'I've been under a lot of strain recently and I didn't mean to sound off at you like that.'

One dark eyebrow rose with complete surprise, then he nodded. 'I accept your apology,' he said in a firm tone. 'But I would like an explanation.'

'I've told you, Brady.' She gave him a tremulous smile. 'I'm afraid I've just been on edge recently, what with worrying about Tom and now the business.' She shrugged slim shoulders.

For a moment there was a look of sympathy in the deep eyes. 'I can understand that.'

A stretched silver-grey limousine rolled up behind them and Brady glanced around and gave a nod towards the chauffeur. 'I have to go, Belle; I have another business appointment,' he said over his shoulder. 'Can I drop you anywhere?'

'No, thanks, I have my car.'

The dark eyes were turned directly on to her again. 'Perhaps we can have that dinner when I get back from France?'

She hesitated. Obviously the only way she was going to succeed in proving her suspicions was by following a different tack. 'Perhaps we can have dinner when we get to France?' She forced herself to say the words in a light, jovial tone.

There was a moment's pause. 'I didn't realise you were planning to come out to Nice.'

'Spur-of-the-moment decision,' she said crisply. 'Hope you don't mind.'

'Why should I mind?' The dark eyes were watchful. 'I'm taking the company jet out on Friday. Do you want to travel with me?'

She nodded. 'That would suit fine.'

'OK, I'll ring to arrange the time. I presume you are at your parents' house?'

She nodded and tried to ignore the terrible feeling of apprehension. Then she watched him walk away towards the limousine, her heart pounding. She hoped to hell that she was doing the right thing. She didn't want to have anything to do with Brady Webster, she certainly didn't want to go to France with him, but what was it her father had said? Keep your friends close and your enemies closer still.

The silver-grey limo pulled out into the steady stream of rush-hour traffic heading out of London. Where was Brady's next meeting? Isabella wondered as she walked towards her car. For a wild moment she contemplated following him, but that was completely crazy.

She opened the door of her red Mercedes and slung her briefcase on the passenger seat. No, she wouldn't get anywhere just trailing around after him. Even if he was going to a Wolf-Chem meeting she could prove nothing.

She sat and drummed her fingers against the steering-wheel. It galled her to think how trusting the other members of the board were towards Brady, but then they didn't know yet that someone had breached security at the French factory, that someone had actually read the secret file on their new perfume.

It was Brady, she just knew it was. He was the only one except for Richard, Claude and her father who had access to that room. But she couldn't say anything, not just yet.

The only way she was going to prove that Brady Webster was guilty of industrial espionage was to get really close to him, gain his confidence. As she sat there the idea began to take shape. It could prove very dangerous, but then there was a lot at stake.

CHAPTER TWO

'YOU are looking a little better today.' Isabella's eyes moved with concern over her father's pale skin. There was a trace of an improvement, a hint of warmer colour in his face, she told herself firmly. Last week he had been so white that he had seemed to merge in with the hospital linen on the bed.

'Rubbish, I look as if I could do with a month in the Caribbean.' Tom Brook struggled to sit up further.

'Maybe you and Mum should go as soon as you feel up to it,' Isabella suggested lightly.

'And what would I do all day?' Tom snapped irritably.

'Follow doctors' orders and relax,' Isabella replied soothingly.

Tom grunted with displeasure. 'I'm a man who has always been busy and active, Belle. All this talk about changing my lifestyle is nonsense. As soon as I feel fit I shall give you a hand with the business.'

'Oh, no, you won't,' Isabella told him firmly. 'Now that Brady is temporarily chairing the board meetings and I'm there to look after your interests you need have nothing further to do with the business until the doctors give you a complete bill of good health.'

'Perhaps I will be able to come to the office in an advisory capacity?' Tom asked bleakly.

'We'll see.' Isabella wasn't about to commit herself to any promises. Her father had been very seriously ill and as far as she was concerned his health had top priority over the business. Doctors had told him to avoid stress, and she was going to make sure the cantankerous man for once in his life followed orders.

'You are a tough little thing on the quiet,' her father said now, but there was more than a hint of affection in his voice. 'You don't know how delighted I am that you agreed to come into the company. It started off as a family concern and it's only right that a member of the family is there to see to things.'

'I'll do my best, Dad,' Isabella said quietly. She had a good idea just how happy it made him seeing her join Brook Mollinar. He had been asking her to come and work for the company ever since she had graduated from university, but Isabella had steadfastly refused.

'You're not regretting coming back to London, are you, Belle?' For a moment her father looked anxious.

'Don't be silly. I've given up a job with a small cosmetics company and now I'm on the board of directors of one of the largest companies in Europe. How could I be sorry?' Isabella assured him hastily. 'In fact I think I'll start looking for an apartment somewhere around the London offices soon.'

'What about your boyfriend? I suppose you are going to miss him. What's his name...? Giles?'

'Julien.' Isabella frowned. 'Brady asked me the same question only yesterday.'

'Did he, now?' Her father grinned. 'Brady listens to me more than I realise,' he said fondly. 'How is he anyhow? I had hoped he would pop in to see me.'

'You're allowed no visitors other than family,' Isabella told him firmly. 'And Brady is the same as ever—utterly infuriating and totally untrustworthy.'

Tom Brook shook his head. 'You and I will always disagree over Brady. I happen to think he's the best thing that ever happened to Brook Mollinar. He's also the reason that you have always refused to work there, isn't he?'

Her father's words took her breath away for a moment. She had thought that she had successfully hidden the real reason for not wanting to work for the company. 'Well…shall we say that his being there has not exactly been an incentive.' She was still evasive on the subject, partly because she was loath to admit that Brady Webster could influence her thinking in any way. 'I just don't like the man.'

'Why? Is it because you've had an affair with him?'

The blunt question made Isabella's cheeks glow with warm colour. 'Certainly not!' What had been between her and that man could hardly be described as an affair, she thought grimly; a mistake would be a more apt description. 'I've told you—I just don't like him. He's untrustworthy; he's a snake.'

Tom Brook grinned. 'You mean he's had a lot of women in his life? Maybe he has changed.'

Isabella snorted. 'Men like him don't change, they just shed their skins.'

Her father looked thoroughly amused now.

'Anyway, I think he's behind the attempt to steal the ideas for our new perfume,' she continued heatedly.

Tom shook his head. 'I refuse to believe that, Isabella.'

'Why? Because the man has been your friend? We'll have to face reality, Tom. Brady is one of the few who have a key to Claude's office, and he has a lot to gain by remaining one step ahead of the perfume development. He could be passing on the information to Wolf-Chem.'

'Absolutely not.' Her father shook his head. 'The man has his reputation to think of; if something like that got out it could ruin him. As well as that, Brady has invested a lot of money into the project; he has a vested interest in seeing that it's a success.'

'But maybe Brady gets a bigger cut of the profits at Wolf-Chem,' Isabella declared stubbornly. 'And let's face it, Dad, the room wasn't broken into; someone used a key and someone knew the combination of the safe. We wouldn't even know there had been someone in there but for the fact that Claude knew the files had been put back in the wrong order. Now that points to an inside job. It's either Brady or Richard, and I can't see Richard doing something like that, can you?'

'No.' Tom shook his head. 'But I still don't believe Brady is responsible.' For a moment he looked worried, and immediately Isabella felt guilty. She was supposed to be cheering him up and not worrying him about business, and here she was discussing a very sensitive subject.

'Anyway, there's no real harm done,' she continued on hastily. 'Claude hasn't finished his work on the perfume, so whoever looked at the file will have been disappointed. I'll just have to make sure that no one is able to breach security again. That's one of the reasons I'm going to fly out there with Brady on Friday.'

'You're going to Nice with Brady?' For a moment her father gave a broad smile. 'That's great, Belle. Are you going to stay at his house?'

Isabella shrugged. 'I think a hotel will be better. Anyway, he hasn't invited me to his home.'

'Oh, but he will. Brady is very fond of you, honey.'

Her father looked happy again, so Isabella bit her tongue on the reply to that.

'I take it you've told Brady that someone's been through Claude's files?' Tom asked now.

Isabella shook her head. 'I haven't told anyone. I can't risk tipping off the culprit, whoever that might be. Once I do that I stand little chance of finding who's responsible.'

'I suppose you're right. But I still think you should tell Brady. You need his help. I would have discussed the whole matter with him except for this damned heart problem.'

The nurse put her head around the door at that moment, saving Isabella from having to make a reply. 'I think it's time that Mr Brook got some more rest,' she said diplomatically.

Isabella nodded and stood up immediately. 'I'm sorry, Dad, I didn't mean to stay so long.' She went across to kiss him.

'You haven't stayed long enough,' Tom told her fondly. 'Perhaps when you get back from France I'll be out of hospital.'

Isabella nodded and bent to kiss him. 'Don't worry about anything. I have it all in hand and I shall call you from France.'

Tom nodded. 'And don't forget, don't allow personal feelings about Brady to cloud rational judgement.'

Those words echoed in Isabella's head as she waited for Brady to pick her up the following afternoon. Was she allowing personal antagonism for the man to cloud her thinking? She sincerely hoped not. She crossed to the window and stared out at the driveway. She was very nervous about seeing him today, apprehensive about the trip to France.

It was a lovely spring day; a breeze was playing with the red tulips on the lawn and stirring the cherry trees so that pink blossom was falling like confetti on the fresh green of the grass. Spring was a time for starting over; everything was new and hopeful with the promise of summer.

Perhaps she should be less harsh in her judgement of Brady, she thought suddenly. Just because he had treated her badly it didn't necessarily make him a criminal. She smiled at the thought and decided to work hard at keeping an open mind. After all, Brady could indeed have changed. Eight years was a very long time.

A long silver limousine pulled into the drive.

'Brady's here, Belle,' her mother called to her from the breakfast-room. There was a note of excitement in her voice that Isabella did not miss. Everyone liked Brady.

'Yes, I know.' Isabella watched the car pull to a halt at the front door. Brady climbed out and looked up at the house. He was wearing a dark suit and a heavy overcoat to keep out the chill that was still in the air. Isabella couldn't help thinking how handsome he looked; she could feel that familiar pull deep inside her as her eyes took in everything about him. She was so busy studying him that she didn't realise for a moment that a woman was stepping out of the car beside him.

She was a willowy blonde, the type with legs that seemed to go on forever. Her hair was loose and long around a face that was expertly made up to emphasise large eyes and pouting red lips. Who on earth was that? Isabella wondered. His girlfriend? His future wife? Her mind seemed to be working overtime on the possibilities as she made her way to open the front door.

She found herself wishing that she had put something a little more interesting on than the black and white checked suit. It had looked correct in the mirror this morning, but, faced with such a beautiful woman in a bright orange loose sweater dress that did nothing to hide the soft curves of her body and the long length of her legs, Isabella suddenly felt dowdy.

'Good morning, Belle.' Brady seemed in good humour as he stepped easily in past her. 'You haven't met Gemma, have you?'

'No.' Isabella's eyes met directly with the other woman's. 'Good morning.'

The woman merely nodded, a cool expression on her classical features.

'Is your mother about?' Brady asked now and then as she appeared out into the hall his face broke into a smile of real pleasure. 'Elizabeth! Nice to see you.'

'How are you keeping, Brady?' Isabella's mother crossed to kiss his cheek. She looked small next to his tall, powerful frame, Isabella thought, and somehow even more delicate than usual. Tom's illness had taken its toll on her. There was a look of strain in the brown eyes, an unusually pale look to the sallow skin, but for all of that she was still an exceptionally attractive woman.

'I'm fine. More to the point, how are you?' he asked with concern.

'Better now that I know Tom will be out of hospital soon,' she said with a smile. 'Have you time to come through and have coffee?'

'I'd love to, but unfortunately we are going to have to dash. I'll take you up on the offer when we come back.' He bent to pick up Isabella's case from next to the hall table. 'You've met my secretary, Gemma Taylor, haven't you, Elizabeth?'

'Yes, I have.' Elizabeth gave the other woman a warm smile.

Secretary? Isabella's lips twisted in dry amusement. Brady could certainly pick them. So much for his being a changed man.

Isabella picked up her jacket. 'I'll ring you tomorrow, Mum. If you need me I've booked a room at the Negresco Hotel in Nice; the number's on the pad by the phone.'

'Booked a room at a hotel?' Brady looked at her, a strange expression in his dark eyes. 'What on earth have you done that for?'

It had been a case of cold feet early this morning. The thought of staying at Brady's house again had conjured up vivid memories, memories that had sent her scuttling towards the phone to make sure she had somewhere else to stay. She shrugged lightly. 'Just to be organised.'

'Well, you can just cancel it,' he said abruptly. 'You are staying at my house.'

'That's very kind of you, Brady—' Isabella started to protest, her voice ice-cool. She didn't care for that dictatorial tone and the prospect of staying at his house was quite frankly alarming her now.

'Nonsense, it's just practical of me. You will be nearer the factory at my place, save me having to send the car down for you every day.'

'Yes, do stay with Brady, dear,' Elizabeth interrupted. 'I think it would be much better, and it will conjure up happy memories of that lovely holiday you had out there years ago. Do you remember?'

Isabella could feel her face flooding with an embarrassed heat. Did she remember...? Hell, she wished that she didn't. She wished that that particular memory had been wiped clear from her mind forever. She looked up and caught Brady's eye. He was remembering it too; she could see the gleam in his dark eyes, the wry twist of his lips, and for a moment she wanted to die.

From somewhere she found the strength to reply. 'Vaguely,' she said in what she hoped was a dismissive tone.

'Only vaguely?' Brady's eyebrow lifted sardonically. 'You do surprise me.'

Isabella flashed him a look of anger. He really was an arrogant, horrible man and he certainly hadn't changed one little bit.

'Well, I can see that I'll have to do something about jogging your memory,' he said as he held the door open for both women.

He was teasing her now and Isabella was definitely not

amused at such audacity. 'I'd rather you didn't, Brady,' she said stiffly. Then she turned to embrace her mother. 'I'll ring you.'

As the limousine swept down the drive towards the main road Isabella was filled with a feeling of deep foreboding. This trip was a mistake; she knew deep inside that she shouldn't be making it.

As the house disappeared from view Isabella turned from waving to her mother and tried hard to dispel the uneasy thoughts. She had to make the trip and it was probably best that she should stay with Brady, it would make it that much easier to keep an eye on him.

It was silent in the car. Brady was seated next to her, reading some notes from a soft leather briefcase. Gemma was sitting opposite and when Isabella glanced over she found the woman staring at her in a rather calculating way, almost as if she was weighing her up.

'What time is our flight?' Isabella asked her conversationally.

'Three o'clock,' Gemma answered bluntly, then glanced at her gold wristwatch. 'You need to make that call to Switzerland, Brady; it's after one now.'

'Right.' Brady spoke without glancing up from his papers. 'Dial the number for me, Gemma.'

The woman opened her leather attaché case and took out a file to check the number before picking up the phone. She spoke in fluent German to whoever answered her call. Isabella couldn't make out too much of what she was saying; she could speak a little German but not enough.

The phone was passed over to Brady and much to Isabella's annoyance he also spoke in German. So there wasn't much chance of her finding out what the call was about.

'Sorry, Belle,' Brady muttered as he finished the call. 'I have a lot of work to get through, so I don't like to waste valuable time. I'm afraid Gemma and I will be working through most of the journey.'

'That's all right.' Isabella shrugged slim shoulders, glad really that she was spared having to make polite conversation. She was surprised that he bothered to apologise.

Isabella revised her opinion of Gemma during the journey. It was very obvious from the speed with which she was taking dictation and ploughing through correspondence that Brady didn't just have her around for decoration; the woman was extremely proficient at her job. But somehow Isabella couldn't bring herself to like her; there was something cold about her, something that made Isabella feel uncomfortable.

The chauffeur left them at the front entrance of the airport and it was a smooth and quick transition getting on the company jet. Then as soon as they got themselves settled into the luxurious seats Brady started work again.

The plane was starting its descent into Nice airport when Brady finally packed away his papers. 'Looks as if the weather's good,' he remarked idly as he glanced out of the window. 'If you're lucky, Gemma, you just might go back to London with a tan.'

For the first time the girl laughed. 'The day I go away with you on a business trip and come back with a tan I'll know that you are softening up.'

'Are you trying to tell me that I'm too tough on you?' Brady asked with amusement.

'Something like that.' The girl patted his arm affectionately. 'But as it's you I'll forgive you.'

Isabella turned her head away from the easy rapport. Women usually did forgive Brady anything, she thought vehemently; that was one of the things that had made him so damn arrogant. But she hadn't forgiven him and she never would.

* * *

She had first met Brady when she was seventeen. Her father had just taken him on the board of directors and he had been invited up to the house for dinner.

Isabella had not been joining them for the meal; she had been invited to a friend's party and had been waiting for her date to arrive and pick her up. When the doorbell had rung she had crossed to open the door, thinking it was for her. Brady had stood outside, looking distinguished in a dark suit that was tailored to his athletic body in a way that seemed to accentuate its powerful lean line. Dark eyes had met hers. 'You must be Isabella.'

She nodded, feeling almost mesmerised by him. Everything about him was perfect, from the deep, husky timbre of his voice to the subtle tang of his expensive cologne. He was her ideal, the type of man that she had dreamed might carry her away on a tide of passion one day.

'I'm Brady Webster; your father is expecting me.' He stepped past her into the hall.

Isabella blinked; this man was a director in her father's company! None of Tom Brook's other business associates looked like him; they were all crusty older men. This man looked like a heart-throb from the movie screen and far too young to have so much power and money. Aware that she was staring at him, she tried very hard to gather her senses and smile politely.

'Come into the lounge, Mr Webster.'

'Brady,' he corrected her with a smile, and those deep eyes moved over her in a sweeping glance.

She was wearing a smoky blue dress that was off the shoulder. It was pretty in a young way, hardly the kind of dress that Brady's girlfriends—heaven forbid he had a wife—would wear. Isabella felt decidedly self-conscious of her appearance; she wished fervently that she had put on something a little more sophisticated, something that didn't emphasise her slender, coltish long legs and her lack of voluptuous curves. And more than anything she wished that she hadn't been wearing her glasses.

Before she had time to show him through to the other room the doorbell rang again. This time it was her boyfriend.

Steve Roland was the same age as her; they were in the same class, studying for their A levels. He was a good-looking young man and he was certainly popular with the other girls at college, yet next to Brady he looked delicate, a mere boy.

Her father came down the stairs just as she had finished introducing them. As he greeted Brady and Steve, Isabella picked up her coat from the cloakroom.

'You are leaving us?' Brady stepped forward and held her coat for her.

'The youngsters are off to an end-of-term party,' her father answered for her.

Isabella felt her cheeks grow hot with embarrassment. Did her father have to make her sound like a ten-year-old?

There was a gleam of amusement in Brady's dark eyes. 'Now you've succeeded in making me feel old, Tom,' he said with laughter in his voice. 'What are you studying, Isabella?'

'French, Italian, English language and Commerce.'

Brady then surprised her by speaking to her in fluent French. 'It's been nice meeting you, Belle,' he said. 'It's a shame you have to dash off.'

For a moment Isabella's heart raced. 'Belle' in French meant beautiful and she had thought that was what he was calling her until she caught the gleam in his eyes and realised that he was just teasing her in a light-hearted way by shortening her name.

She had answered him back in French. 'You speak the language well, *monsieur.*'

He shrugged. 'I hope so. I have a house just outside Cannes and I spend a lot of time out there.'

Steve was growing impatient—she could see him glancing at his watch out of the corner of her eye—and with regret she wound up the conversation. 'We really must go. Hope to see you soon, Brady.'

'I'm sure you will. *Au revoir*,' he said in that deep, beautiful tone.

Isabella did not enjoy her evening one little bit. Her eyes travelled continually to her watch and her thoughts to Brady.

At eleven she made the excuse that she had a headache and asked Steve to take her home. He agreed readily; she didn't realise exactly why he had been so happy to leave early until they stopped outside her house.

Much to her delight Brady's car was still in the drive. She wished Steve a hurried goodnight and reached for the car door-handle, but he had other ideas.

'Don't rush off, Isabella.' He caught hold of her wrist and she turned to look at him questioningly.

He had caught her off guard and the next moment he had pulled her into his arms and was kissing her with a fervour that took her breath away.

She tried to pull away from him, but his hand held her firmly while his mouth plundered hers in a way that completely threw her into panic.

'Don't, Steve.' She pushed at him, but it was like pushing against a rock.

'Relax,' he murmured, his hands getting more and more insistent as they moved roughly over her body.

It was then that the door behind her opened and a coolly sardonic voice spoke.

Steve released her immediately and Isabella turned flustered eyes up to Brady's dark face.

'Sorry to interrupt,' he said briskly, 'but your car is hemming me in, Steve.'

'Sorry, sir.' Steve was immediately apologetic and a little red in the face.

'That's OK, just move it.' Brady's eyes noted Isabella's look of distress and he held out a hand to help her as she turned to get out of the car.

Somehow she managed to say a shaky goodbye to Steve, then his car turned and drove away from them, leaving her alone on the drive with Brady.

'Trying to take liberties, was he?' There was a note of dry humour in the deep voice.

Isabella cringed with embarrassment. 'He was just saying goodnight.'

Brady smiled. 'I don't blame him a bit; you are a very lovely young woman.'

The compliment made her heart turn somersaults.

'Though I do feel a little sorry for him.'

She frowned. 'Why on earth should you feel sorry for him?'

'Unrequited love can be no joy.' He smiled. 'Although they say that even love unreturned has its rainbow.' The inky blackness of the night seemed to envelop them in a moment of intimacy as Brady placed an arm around her slender shoulders and walked with her towards the front door.

'Steve is not in love with me; we're just friends,' she told him lightly as they stopped outside it.

'Then the man's a fool.' Brady smiled at her and touched her cheek. 'Goodnight, Belle.'

Those words and the touch of his hand lived with her over the next few months, although she saw little of Brady.

He was a busy man, spending most of his time in Switzerland and France, flying back to London only for the occasional board meeting or when something urgent came up. On those occasions Isabella usually invented some excuse to go up to the offices just so that she could see him for a few minutes.

She couldn't believe her luck when he was in town at the time of her eighteenth birthday.

Her father threw a big party for her at the house. Everyone was invited—all the old family friends and members of the board as well as college friends. When Brady's card arrived saying he would be able to attend she flew into an excited panic. She took such time and trouble with what to wear.

She could still remember that dress vividly. Pale pink silk, cut exquisitely to expose creamy shoulders and a long neckline. She wore no jewellery and left off her glasses...which was a big mistake as it turned out.

Brady was one of the last guests to arrive. Isabella had tried to stay near the door area so that she could see when he arrived, but it was an impossibility. People kept claiming her attention, and it was necessary to mingle. She was right over the other side of the room when he finally walked in, and she wouldn't have known except that her father was standing next to her.

'Here is Brady now,' he said with a smile.

She glanced across the crowded room, but Brady's dark figure was a mere fuzzy blur to her eyes. With shaking hands she put down her champagne and excused herself from the people around her to go and welcome him.

'Belle, you look wonderful.' His eyes were warm as they took in her appearance. 'Happy birthday. I left a small package for you out with the other presents on the hall table.'

'Thanks, Brady.' Her smile was shy. 'And thanks for coming.'

'My pleasure. You haven't met Bobby, have you?'

Isabella turned and with a shock noticed the stunning redhead who had arrived with him.

'Roberta Webb.' The woman smiled and held out a hand towards her. She was about Brady's age—twenty-eight or -nine—and radiantly beautiful in a black dress that set off her dramatic colouring to perfection.

'Pleased to meet you.' Somehow Isabella gathered herself together, but it was a supreme effort.

After that her party seemed flat. Oh, she had danced with her men friends from college, laughed at their jokes, but all the time she was conscious of the fact that the man she wanted to be with was with someone else.

That night, when everyone had gone home, she found the present that Brady had left for her—a beautiful string of pearls.

Pearls for tears, she thought drily now as the plane bumped down on the runway. She had certainly cried enough over the man. If only she had left things there, if only she hadn't continued to pursue him after that party, it wouldn't have been so bad. But unfortunately even after seeing the danger signs she had still wanted him and she hadn't given up until he had succeeded in making a complete fool of her. Well, never again, she vowed silently. Never again would Brady Webster get the opportunity to hurt her.

CHAPTER THREE

THE house was exactly as she remembered it. Spacious, elegant and beautiful, it was everything you would imagine a millionaire's house in the South of France to look like.

It was set up in the hills near Old Grimaud and its front windows looked out over the rolling countryside towards the sparkle of the blue Mediterranean. The sun was setting now, giving a rosy glow to the fields full of regimented rows of vines. It looked like a Cézanne painting, Isabella thought as she turned away from the view. No wonder French Impressionists had painted such superb pictures, with such a lot of inspirational beauty surrounding them.

She looked around her bedroom. It was the same one that she had stayed in last time she had visited. Isabella wondered if it was Brady's idea of a joke to put her in here again. After all, he had so many other rooms to choose from. Why put her somewhere that would evoke bitter memories? Unless that was his specific intention. Irritated by the thought, Isabella went to sit down at the dressing-table to finish her make-up.

Maybe it was coincidence that she was back in the same room, she told her reflection sensibly. After all, it was eight years ago since she had been here; he could in all possibility have forgotten where she'd stayed. She wished fervently that she could forget as easily.

She applied a soft petal-pink to her lips and sat back to study her reflection. Her skin was a little too pale; her blue eyes looked a deeper shade of sapphire with the coloured

contact lenses. There had been a time when she couldn't
wear lenses—they had made her sensitive eyes stream with
tears—but she had persevered, especially after Brady had
dented her pride.

She stood up and picked up her bag to go downstairs.
If only she could stop thinking about the past. She had
come here for a specific reason; she had to have all her
wits about her, and clouding them with emotive memories
wasn't going to help. Isabella stopped by the door, a
thought suddenly striking her. Was that why Brady had
put her in this room? Was it to try and distract her thoughts
away from business? Her mouth set in a grim line; if that
was so, then Brady was going to have a very rude awak-
ening. She was no longer a naïve girl who could be easily
flattered and easily distracted. She was well able to deal
with a man like Brady on his own tough terms.

She found him in the lounge, sharing a pre-dinner drink
with Gemma.

'There you are, Belle.' He stood up from the settee and
crossed to the drinks cabinet to get her a sherry. 'We were
wondering where you were hiding yourself.'

'I wasn't hiding.' Isabella glared at him, angry at his
choice of words. 'I was unpacking.'

He handed her the drink. 'Sit down and make yourself
at home.' He waved to the settee where Gemma was sitting. 'Madame Dupont will be calling us in for dinner at
any moment.'

'Madame Dupont is still with you?' Isabella glanced up
in surprise.

'More's the pity,' Gemma mumbled under her breath.

That made Isabella smile. She remembered being a little
frightened of the woman when she had first met her, then
she had discovered that under that crusty exterior there was
a heart of gold. Gemma had obviously failed to discover
this.

'Yes, she is now sixty-five years old and she looks terrific. No sign of her ever retiring, which suits me just fine, as I consider her a member of my family, and, as you no doubt remember, she is a first-rate cook. I would be lost without her.' Brady poured himself another whisky and came to sit opposite them. 'Cheers, here's to a successful trip.'

Isabella raised her glass. Hopefully it would be successful; hopefully she would prove Brady was the one who had gone through Claude's notes. But how was she going to go about it? she mused.

Madame Dupont interrupted her thoughts as she came in to call them for dinner. She hadn't changed at all, Isabella thought with surprise. Her figure was still extremely trim, her grey hair still neat and short around a rather angular face. Her features softened with a smile when she saw Isabella.

'You look beautiful, *chérie*,' she said, her eyes noting the subtle changes in the younger woman. 'Very sophisticated now, very chic. Is that not so?' she asked Brady, making Isabella cringe with embarrassment.

'She certainly is,' Brady agreed smoothly. 'I barely recognised Belle when I saw her again after all these years.'

'It has been too long,' the housekeeper said with a shake of her head as she led the way through to the dining-room.

They ate in the dining-room at the back of the house, which looked out at the terrace and the large swimming-pool. Isabella sat facing the windows and every time she glanced up at that sparkling blue pool she was reminded vividly of a warm summer's night when Brady had held her body against his in the cool blue silk of the water.

'Belle?' Brady's voice penetrated her consciousness and she realised he had been speaking to her and she hadn't heard a word he was saying.

'Sorry, Brady, I was miles away.' She could feel colour

steal into her cheeks as he smiled. Did he guess just where her thoughts had been?

'I asked if you would like coffee in the lounge.'

'Yes, that would be nice.' She got to her feet, relieved to be leaving that view of the floodlit pool.

Gemma, who had spoken little during the meal, suddenly spoke in French to Brady. 'Perhaps I could have a moment alone with you, Brady; there is something I would like to discuss.'

'I'll leave the two of you, then.' Isabella also spoke in French, getting a reply in before Brady. She noticed the other woman's look of surprise with a feeling of annoyance. Obviously Gemma had not realised she could speak French. Her dislike of the other woman deepened; how rude of her to try to isolate her like that. With her head held high she left them.

Instead of going back to the lounge she made her way to the kitchen to speak to Madame Dupont.

The woman was delighted to see her. 'Sit down, sit down.' She waved her towards the large wooden table. 'We will take coffee together.'

Isabella sat down with a feeling of relief; she would much rather sit in here with the delightful Frenchwoman than sit with Brady and Gemma.

She looked about the kitchen as she waited for the woman to sit down with their coffee. She had always liked this kitchen; it had rustic charm like a country kitchen where one would expect to find pheasants hanging ready to be plucked. She smiled at the idle thought; the only thing hanging in here was a bunch of dried flowers that Madame Dupont had arranged on the shelf over the gleaming brass range. They scented the air with lavender and camomile.

'So, it is nice to see you back.' The woman put the blue

china cups on the table and poured the strong coffee. 'You look happier than when you left.'

'I should hope so.' Isabella's lips twisted wryly. She had been in a very sorry state the day she had left here. If it hadn't been for Madame Dupont's kindness she would have been even worse. 'You were very kind to me, *madame*,' she said now.

The woman gave a Gallic shrug. 'I know what it is like to have a broken heart.'

'I didn't have a broken heart,' Isabella corrected her quickly, then, catching the gleam in the other woman's eyes, she smiled. 'My ego was a little bruised.'

'But now you are a confident young woman once more.' The housekeeper smiled. 'You have a nice young man in your life?'

Isabella smiled as she thought about Julien. He was a nice young man; it was a good description. But, as to the fact of having him in her life, that was stretching things. She shrugged. 'I have a good friend,' she said cautiously. 'He's French; I met him when I was working in Paris.'

'Ah.' The woman smiled knowingly. 'I think you will be happy with a French lover.'

Isabella's cheeks flared with a delicate colour and she was about to tell the woman that Julien was not her lover when they were interrupted by a voice from the doorway.

'I don't think you should be filling Belle's head with such nonsense,' Brady said crisply.

Isabella turned startled eyes to where he stood in the doorway. How long had he been standing there? she wondered uncomfortably.

'It is not nonsense, it is a well known fact, Monsieur Webster.' The Frenchwoman was not one bit daunted by Brady's presence; in fact she gave Isabella a knowing wink as she rose to her feet to get the coffee-pot for him. 'I presume you and Mademoiselle Gemma are ready for coffee now?'

'Yes, please. We are in the lounge.' Brady's dark eyes lingered thoughtfully for a moment on Isabella. It was a strange look, a look that was almost angry. Although why he would be angry with her she had no idea. 'Are you coming to join us, Belle?' His voice was pleasant enough, dispelling the idea in Isabella's head.

She finished her coffee and stood up. 'No, thanks, Brady. I think I'll turn in for the night if you don't mind.'

'Not at all,' Brady said smoothly. 'I do want to leave for the factory early tomorrow.'

Isabella nodded. 'Good night, *madame*, thank you for the coffee.'

'You are welcome, *chérie*.'

As Isabella made her way down the corridor she could hear the housekeeper extolling her virtues. 'A lovely young woman,' she said in a meaningful voice. 'A pity you let her escape you. Now she has a French lover and it is too late for you.'

Despite her embarrassment at such a comment Isabella had to smile at the woman's audacity. She certainly didn't believe in standing on ceremony when she spoke to her employer.

Brady merely laughed at that. 'You sound more like my dear mother every day, *madame*. And I'll have you know that there is an old proverb that says, "It is not lost that comes at last".'

Isabella frowned. What on earth was that supposed to mean? As she went through the door back into the hallway she could hear him laugh again. It was a deep, warm sound; obviously Brady was having some kind of a joke at her expense, Isabella thought furiously as she let the door slam.

Isabella couldn't sleep that night. Her mind was racing

around in circles. It seemed so strange being back here again after eight years. Sitting in the kitchen tonight with Madame Dupont had made her remember so vividly the naïve teenager she had been then.

She got up and switched on the air-conditioning. Was it a very warm night? she wondered. Or was it just stuffy in here? She opened the window next to her bed and stood looking out over the dark garden and down over the countryside towards the sea. Surprisingly for early May it *was* a warm night. The sky was bright with stars and the crickets were making a noisy whirling sound like a generator that was constantly turning on. She took a deep breath of air; it was scented with the fragrance of night-scented stock and lavender.

There was something exciting about the South of France; she had felt it the last time she was here. It was a feeling in the air, a feeling that heightened the senses. Maybe it was just the beauty of it all that took your breath away, or maybe there really was a magical quality to the air. Was that the reason she had acted so foolishly last time she had been here?

The idea was so absurd that she had to smile. It wasn't the wine and it wasn't Brady Webster, it was the air that had made her so reckless! The amusement faded and she turned away from the window. It was the first time that she had been able to smile about that awful incident, and even now the humour of it was twisting back into a horrible reality of just how foolish she had been.

She got back into bed and tried to close her mind to the memory. Everyone makes mistakes, she told herself rationally. She tried to think of Julien and how sweet he had been to her in Paris. She lay back against the pillows and tried to picture his blond, blue-eyed gentle face. Instead a picture of Brady rose up in front of her eyes, the dark eyes glittering, his mouth twisted in a scornful way. That was the way he had looked at her the day he had sent her away. Maybe she had deserved his scorn; maybe it had been all her fault.

Soon after her eighteenth birthday Isabella started at university. She had got excellent results in her A levels and her parents were thrilled and very proud of her. Isabella was pleased too; after all, this was what she had wanted. She had studied hard, so that she could go to university and hopefully leave with the high qualifications to be able to follow in her father's footsteps. Why then did she feel unsettled? Why couldn't she get Brady out of her mind?

She found it almost impossible to concentrate. Thoughts of Brady invaded her mind at the most inconvenient times. In the middle of a lecture, in the middle of an assignment, his face would rear up in her mind and she would find herself wondering if he was still with that glamorous redhead, if he was serious about her. Then as the summer holidays approached she concocted a plan to get nearer to him.

She asked her father if he would find her a summer job at his factory in the South of France. She reasoned that it would be excellent experience for her to work in an environment that she was actually training for at university, and it would improve her French.

He thought it an excellent idea. Tom Brook very much wanted his only daughter to join the business, and it would give her a grounding in exactly what went on at the factory.

'I'll stay at the hotel where you usually stay when you go out there on business,' she said innocently.

'Nonsense.' Tom squashed that idea immediately, just as she had hoped he would. 'I'll ask Brady if you can stay with him. His house is very near to the factory, and besides, I think you would be safer there.'

Safer there! That was a joke, she thought wryly now...
How wrong he had been.

She remembered how Brady had picked her up at Nice
airport and had driven her back along the Corniche D'or
in his open-topped Mercedes. The sun had blazed down
out of a clear azure-blue sky and the wind had blown her
blonde hair into a riot of curls around her young face as
she had laughed with him, flirted with him even. She had
been so excited, so sure that she was in heaven with Brady
Webster.

Her job at the factory had been menial, but it had given
her a chance to work beside Claude and observe his ge-
nius. She had seen little of Brady during the days, but in
the evening they had usually shared dinner together. There
had been no sign of another girlfriend for a while, no mention of the beautiful Roberta. Isabella had started to grow
more confident that Brady was attracted to her. He'd
treated her with gentle humour, always courteous, always
correct. Then one day he had kissed her.

It had happened quite spontaneously. Isabella had been
helping him to reorganise his office one Saturday afternoon
and she had bent down to help him pick up some papers
he had dropped on the floor. As they straightened their
heads had bumped.

'Oh!' Half laughing, half crying, she rubbed her head
ruefully. 'That hurt!'

'Sorry, sweetheart.' He reached across and rubbed her
head with a concerned hand. 'Where does it hurt?' He
pushed her blonde silky hair back from her forehead and
stroked her skin.

The touch of his hands against her skin was electric.
The pain was forgotten as impulsively she took a step forward.

'Brady.' She whispered his name and his hand moved
from her forehead to her cheek. His eyes were on her lips

and she moistened them nervously. His kiss took her breath away; gentle, tender, it made her melt towards him.

He stopped just as abruptly as he had started. His hand on her shoulder, he moved firmly back. 'I'm sorry, Belle, I shouldn't have done that.'

Before she had a chance to regain her breath and tell him she didn't mind a bit he left the room.

Brady went out later that afternoon and he didn't arrive home in time for dinner. In fact he didn't arrive back until nearly midnight, and Isabella had gone to bed.

Their relationship seemed to change after that. Instead of the good-humoured banter that they had once enjoyed, their conversation was stilted and filled with an undercurrent that made Isabella awkward around him. She longed to tell him how she felt about him, how she had longed for his kiss, but she never dared. Then before she had a chance Roberta arrived.

It was supposed to be a fleeting visit, but in fact the woman stayed for two weeks. Isabella was filled with a terrible jealousy of the other woman. She tried very hard not to feel like that, but it was hard when she watched the glamorous redhead enjoying the laughing, easy relationship with Brady that she had once had. Dinners were three-somes now, and indeed some nights Isabella was left to her own devices when the couple were late home and stopped for dinner in town.

Isabella wasn't sure if the couple were lovers or not, but what she lacked in information she more than made up for with imagination. At night she would lie and imagine them in each other's arms. One night, when sleep, as usual, was evading her, she got up, put her dressing-gown on, and went down to the kitchen for a drink.

A bottle of red wine was uncorked and sitting on one of the counters. She lifted it up and, getting a glass, brought it out to the terrace to sit and get some fresh air.

The night air was warm and sultry, the red wine like nectar to her ruffled nerves. She drank one glass and leaned her head back against the padded chair as she looked down over the pool and the surrounding beauty of the garden swathed in silver moonlight.

'What are you doing out here, Belle?' Brady's deep voice made her jump.

She glanced up and saw him standing next to her. He was wearing nothing but a pair of swimming-trunks, and there was a towel slung casually over his broad shoulders.

'Just getting some air.' Her voice trembled a little; her eyes had difficulty dragging themselves away from the lean, powerful line of his body.

'How much of that stuff have you drunk?' He nodded to the bottle sitting next to her.

'Only a glass.' A defiant spark of anger lit her eyes. 'I am eighteen, Brady; that makes it quite legal for me to have a drink,' she told him sardonically.

'I'm well aware of how old you are.' He ground the words out, sounding half amused, half angry.

'Well, if it's not my age that you are worried about, is it the price of the bottle of wine?' It was a ridiculous question to ask a man of Brady's wealth, but she was angry with him for ignoring her for so long; her pride was hurt and she wanted to strike out at him. 'If so, I'm sure my father will reimburse you.' Her voice was arrogant, as was the tilt of her head as she looked up at him.

Instead of rising to the bait, he merely laughed. 'I'm pleased to hear it,' he said with amused sarcasm. 'I'll send him an itemised bill, shall I? At the top of it I'll have the charge for the inconvenience of dealing with a spoilt teenager.'

Isabella was furious; her eyes sparkled with rage as she got to her feet. 'How dare you speak to me like that?' She practically spat the words at him.

'Oh, I dare to do anything. In fact…' Before she realised what was happening he had taken her glasses from her nose, lifted her up into strong arms, and tossed her into the swimming-pool.

The shock of hitting that water made her body momentarily rigid and she went right under, swallowing great gulps of it and then struggling as she became tangled with her night-clothes.

Brady was with her in a moment and brought her safely to the side.

It seemed to take ages for her coughing to subside; she felt as if she had swallowed half the pool. When she was able to catch her breath she could only stare at him reproachfully.

'You deserved that, young lady,' was all he said.

He was probably right, she had deserved it. Looking back on the incident when she had been in Paris, she had been bound to agree that at eighteen she had been somewhat spoilt. Standing on her own two feet in a foreign city had soon knocked that out of her, however. Maybe she had deserved being thrown in the pool. But she certainly hadn't deserved what had come next. She hadn't deserved to be so humiliated by him then discarded like some old dish rag.

One moment she had been gasping for breath, the next she had gasped for a completely different reason. Suddenly she had become aware of Brady's hands resting around the narrow span of her waist, the close proximity of his body.

'Brady?' She looked up at him, her heart beating wildly, desire flaring through her in hot, pulsating waves. She ran her hands over the smoothness of his bare shoulders and instinctively pressed close to him.

She heard him draw in a breath, then his lips blazed a heated trail over the cool wetness of her skin.

The blue of the pool and the inky black of the sky

seemed to merge in a wild blur of colour as his hands travelled for a moment over the slender curves of her breasts to her hips. Then together they glided through the soft cool silk of the water to the other side of the pool and he found the light switch that illuminated the water and flicked it off. The water was now lit only by the silver of moonlight as Brady pulled her up and out, to carry her back to her room.

In Isabella's romantically naïve mind, she had thought that the way Brady had kissed her meant that he cared deeply for her. How innocent she had been, brought up in a sheltered world where she had been given everything she ever wanted. Brady had been her first taste of reality.

When he reached her room he placed her down on the floor and for a moment she clung to him, her arms curved around his neck, her wet body pressed close against his. 'Brady, I think I love you.' Her voice was no more than a husky murmur in the silence of the night as gently she opened her heart to him. For a moment she thought he hadn't heard her; he made no immediate reply. Then he reached up and pulled her hands away from him and stepped firmly back from her.

'Get some sleep, Belle.' His voice was almost abrasively rough. 'We'll discuss this in the morning.' Then he was gone, leaving her standing in the centre of the room, her body trembling, tears trickling down her cheeks.

Isabella spent a sleepless night, her mind racing over and over the incident in the pool. The way he had kissed and caressed her had been so wonderful that she felt sure he had some feelings for her. Why, then, hadn't he answered her properly when she had told him how she felt? Why had he left her so abruptly? Perhaps he was bothered by the age-gap between them. She tossed and turned until the early hours of the morning, then fell into a tense and restless sleep.

She got up at seven the following morning and showered and dressed in one of her most attractive dresses. Despite the light make-up she had applied, her skin was pale and waxen, her eyes shadowed from the previous night. With a heavy sigh she turned and made her way downstairs. Part of her was dreading seeing Brady after last night. She felt self-conscious about the way she had responded so eagerly to his kisses, the declaration of love. Yet there was still a little ray of hope that he felt the same way towards her.

Her heart pounded heavily against her breast as she reached the hallway and saw the door of Brady's study ajar. That meant he was already in there; he always kept that door firmly closed when he wasn't in or if he didn't wish to be disturbed. With a feeling of nervous anticipation she went over and tapped on the door.

Brady had already started his day's work. There was a pile of reports spread in front of him on the desk and he was deeply engrossed in them as she walked in.

'Ah, Belle.' He glanced up at her and ran a distracted hand through short dark hair. 'Sit down, I won't be a moment.' He waved her towards the chair opposite as he bent his head to finish a particular file he had been working on.

Isabella's limbs felt as heavy as lead as she walked towards the chair. She hadn't known what kind of reception she would get from Brady this morning, but she certainly hadn't expected this kind of cold indifference.

'Sorry.' Brady put down his pen and then glanced across at her. His dark eyes noted the shadows under her large blue eyes and the pallor of her skin, and for once he looked almost uncertain, as if he just didn't know what to say. Then he spoke, and it became clear that Brady was a lot of things, but uncertain was not one of them.

'Now, then, Belle.' His voice was crisp and decisive. 'I think that it is time you went back to London.'

Isabella swallowed and tried very hard not to allow the emotions inside her to show on her face. Bewildered and very hurt, she nevertheless managed to speak in a level tone. 'Do you mind telling me why?'

One dark eyebrow lifted. 'I'm surprised you really have to ask.' There was a note of impatience in the deep voice now. 'Look, Belle, please don't make this any harder than it is. I will ring through to the airline and get you booked on a flight for this afternoon. I'm sorry, but this is the way it has to be.'

Brady sounded anything but sorry; his manner was brusque yet very controlled, his eyes cool and watchful. Isabella wanted to cry suddenly as the reality of what he was saying started to sink in. 'What about last night?' Her voice wasn't quite as steady now, but she had to ask the question, she had to know exactly what was going through his mind.

'For heaven's sake, girl, do you really want me to spell it out?' His voice rasped against her delicate nerves and suddenly there was a blazing, furious light in his dark eyes. 'Last night I kissed you and I could very easily have made love to you, but it would have been a casual fling…it would have meant nothing. You are a young girl with university and a good career in front of you; I suggest you go and get on with it.'

For a moment searing heat scorched Isabella's cheeks as humiliation washed through her. That he should tell her so bluntly that he cared nothing about her, that he didn't even find her particularly attractive, hurt her like crazy. Without a word she stood up and raced from the room, her body burning with the shame of it all. She practically collided with Roberta in the hallway, but she was too upset even to apologise to the other woman as she ran up the stairs towards the sanctuary of her room.

She packed her case in a kind of frenzy of anger and

unhappiness. Everything was thrown in haphazardly, her mind whirling in confusion. Then she sat on the edge of her bed, not knowing what to do. Brady didn't have any feelings for her; that one fact kept running through her thoughts again and again. She remembered how she had professed her love for him and cringed with the awful embarrassment of it all. How he must have laughed at her last night.

There was a tap at her bedroom door and immediately panic ran through her in case it was Brady, but it was Roberta who put her head around the door. 'Mind if I come in?' she enquired silkily.

Isabella did mind. She felt in no fit state to talk to anyone, least of all Roberta Webb, but good manners prevailed and she forced herself to say no.

'You have packed, I see.' The woman's sharp eyes lighted on the suitcase immediately.

'Yes, it's time I was going back to London.' Isabella forced herself to speak calmly, but it was a tremendous effort.

'Yes, Brady told me.' Roberta smiled at her and for a moment Isabella imagined a gleam of triumph in the other woman's eyes.

How much had Brady told her? she wondered and felt like curling up into a small ball and dying of mortification. She could just imagine them both having a good laugh at her naïveté. Perhaps Brady had left her last night and gone straight to Roberta's room to share the joke with her. All sorts of thoughts raced through Isabella's head, driven by sheer anguish.

The woman's next words confirmed her worst fears. 'I just came in to wish you all the best, Isabella,' she purred throatily. 'And maybe we will see you here for the wedding.'

'What wedding?' Isabella waited with a feeling of utter dread for the answer.

'Why, Brady's and mine, of course.' The woman looked at her with a puzzled expression in her eyes. 'Didn't you know that Brady and I have an understanding?'

Isabella shrugged slim shoulders. She felt utterly wretched now and such a complete fool.

Roberta frowned. 'I can't think why he hasn't told you, darling.' She shrugged. 'Who can understand a man's mind?' The words were spiked with a certain gleam of humour. 'Well, I just want to wish you *bon voyage*, as they say.' Then with a brilliant smile she moved towards the door. 'I believe Madame Dupont is going to drive you to the airport at two o'clock,' she finished casually.

Isabella hoped not to see Brady again before she left. Her heart was sore and her emotions tremulous, to say the least. But it was a forlorn hope as he did appear just as she was getting into the car with Madame Dupont.

He leaned indolently against the side of the car and looked down at her through the open window. 'I wish you all the best, Belle,' he murmured gently.

Isabella continued to stare straight ahead. She didn't dare to glance at him for fear of breaking down and making herself a complete laughing-stock.

'I'll explain to Claude that you have had to leave because of a pressing engagement in London,' he continued briskly.

'Thanks.' There was a note of bitter irony in her voice that did not escape him.

He reached out a hand and touched the side of her face. '*Au revoir*, Belle,' he murmured softly.

She flinched from his touch and sent a frantic look at Madame Dupont. The woman nodded and started up the engine and slowly the car pulled down the drive. Isabella never glanced back once.

The journey to the airport was made in near silence. Isabella had felt betrayed, humiliated. The trip was very different from when she had arrived. Then she had laughed all the way, Brady at her side, her hopes soaring. Now silent tears were welling up inside; she was in black despair.

Madame Dupont embraced her warmly at the airport. Isabella wondered what she thought about her hasty departure; did she realise that Brady was sending her forcibly home?

As if reading her thoughts, the older woman shook her head sadly. 'No man is worth such a depression, *chérie*,' she said gently. 'You are a beautiful, intelligent young woman and, although you don't realise it, now you have the world at your feet.'

Isabella tried to smile through the shimmer of her tears.

'That is right, *chérie*. Hold your head high and know your own worth.'

The lesson had been a hard one to learn. But Isabella had held her head high as she walked on to that plane. She would survive, and no one would ever hurt her like that again.

Isabella tossed and turned and hardly slept all night. She was up at seven, glad to stand under the powerful jet of the shower and wash away the tension and the memories.

She dressed in a cool lemon dress and then surveyed herself in the mirror. She looked pale, but there was a defiant sparkle in her blue eyes. She had learnt her lesson where Brady was concerned and she could hold her head high. She had graduated from university with top honours; she was a power to be reckoned with. She nodded briskly at her reflection and turned to leave the room; she was ready for anything Brady could throw at her.

She found him in the breakfast-room with Gemma. She

was going through the morning correspondence with him and they were both drinking coffee. It looked extremely cosy; Isabella couldn't help wondering if Gemma spent the nights with Brady as well as the days.

'Good morning, Belle, and a lovely morning it is.' Brady reached cheerfully for the coffee-pot and poured her a drink.

He seemed in very good spirits, Isabella thought darkly, full of the joys of spring; Gemma was obviously flavour of the month.

'Did you sleep well?' His eyes moved over her features in a detailed survey that was most disconcerting.

'Yes, thank you.' It was a downright lie and he probably knew it; she looked washed-out.

Gemma passed over two letters to Brady. 'From Wolf-Chem,' she said briskly. 'One's marked urgent; it's something to do with the new perfume.'

'Thanks.' Instead of reading them, Brady put them into his briefcase, which was sitting on the empty chair beside him.

Isabella watched this with interest. 'Wolf-Chem are also working on a new perfume, I take it?' she asked in what she hoped was a casual tone.

'Of course; as you know, they are branching into cosmetics.' Brady looked over at her with a frown. 'I believe we have already discussed this matter at the board meeting.'

'Yes.' Isabella sipped her coffee, her manner relaxed. They hadn't discussed it nearly enough for her liking, but she would bide her time. 'When are you leaving for the factory?' She changed the subject. She didn't want to alert Brady about her suspicions just yet, not until she had some vital proof.

'As soon as you are ready,' Brady answered in a clipped

tone as he turned his attention back to some other letters that Gemma was handing across to him.

Isabella finished her coffee and picked up her bag. 'In that case,' she said crisply, 'let's be on our way.'

The factory was situated about ten minutes' drive away into the mountains. It stood alone in the scented air and was skilfully built to blend in with the beauty of its surroundings. Everything was just as Isabella remembered it, from the factory floor to the gleaming modern offices above; there had been little change.

Claude met them in the entrance hall and greeted them with great enthusiasm. He still looked for all the world like an absent-minded professor, Isabella thought. He was about fifty years of age with a shock of unruly white hair and he wore a white laboratory coat over his suit. The appearance was completely deceptive; there was nothing absent-minded about Claude. He was a most brilliant chemist, top in his field, and the company thought themselves very lucky to have him.

'Mademoiselle Brook, how nice to see you again.' He shook Isabella warmly by the hand. 'How is your father? We have all been most concerned.'

'Tom is progressing slowly,' Isabella told him. 'We expect him out of hospital soon.'

'I am so pleased, although we were all sad to hear he might be retiring now.' As he spoke, Claude turned and led them up to the offices on the top floor. 'Who would have thought when you visited us so many years ago that you would return in such circumstances?' he murmured contemplatively as the lift doors closed on them.

'Yes, you never know what is around the next corner,' Brady remarked drily.

Isabella glanced over at him and their eyes met. Did he resent her presence? she wondered. Just what was running through that sharp mind of his? The dark eyes were deep and unfathomable, his face an unemotional mask.

'I think you and I should have dinner tonight, Belle,' he said suddenly.

Isabella was taken completely aback for a moment. She hadn't been expecting a dinner invitation and certainly not one issued like some kind of a command in front of Gemma and Claude.

'I don't think tonight will be very suitable, Brady.' She angled her chin up firmly and forced herself not to look away from his eyes. She didn't want him to think that she was intimidated by him.

'Why?' he asked calmly.

Aware that Gemma and Claude were listening, Isabella felt most uncomfortable. 'Well...I have some important phone calls to make,' she said lamely.

'You can make them earlier,' Brady said decisively. The lift doors opened and they all stepped out into the corridor. 'Ring and made a reservation at JCA's, please, Gemma.'

Isabella felt furious. She did not want to have dinner out with Brady, but she could hardly make a big fuss about it in front of Gemma and Claude. She noticed that Gemma was not looking too pleased by the order either.

Brady strode ahead of them down the corridor and opened a door to the left. 'This is Tom's office, Belle. I suggest you busy yourself in here today. I know that a lot of his paperwork is still sitting unfinished from his last visit.'

Isabella glared at him. How dared this man issue commands at her as if she were his secretary? She was now representing a major shareholder in the business and she was a member of the board, so she expected to be treated with a little respect, not ordered around. Before she had a chance to object, however, Brady was marching away from

her and down to his office, Gemma practically running to
keep up with him.

The man was totally infuriating, Isabella thought with a
shake of her head. Infuriating and worrying. Why was he
so insistent that she go out to dinner with him tonight?
The question made her very nervous indeed. Brady was
up to something; there was some calculating reason running around in that sharp brain of his, she was sure of it.

CHAPTER FOUR

THE day seemed to drag by. Brady hadn't been joking
when he said that Tom had left a lot of work unfinished.
There was a mountain of paperwork on his desk and it
took most of the morning and the afternoon before she had
managed to put it all in order with the help of her father's
secretary, Nadine.

She took a break at about four and went in search of
Claude. She had some important questions to ask him,
questions that she couldn't have asked in front of Brady.

She found him in his laboratory, entering notes on a
chart. Thankfully he was alone.

'Ah, *mademoiselle*, this is a nice surprise.' The man's
eyes lit up. 'What can I do for you?'

'I wanted to speak to you about the breach in security
last month.'

The man nodded gravely. 'I spoke to your father about
it just before he was taken ill. As the room and the files
hadn't been broken into we decided it might be someone
who has keys. A very disturbing matter.'

'Yes, it certainly is,' Isabella sighed. 'What measures
have been taken to see that it doesn't happen again?'

Claude smiled sadly. 'Your father changed the security
system before he left. I believe it was his last duty at Brook
Mollinar before his heart attack.'

Isabella nodded her head. Poor Tom had only just returned from France when he had to be rushed to hospital.
'Perhaps you would give me a detailed outline of the se-

curity measures that are taken now,' she asked crisply, trying to keep her mind away from the worry of her father's health.

'Certainly.' Claude waved her through to the other room. 'If you would step through to my office.'

They moved through to his private domain, and Claude nodded towards the vault in the corner. 'I can assure you that it is top of the range; even the most professional of criminals would find it hard to penetrate.'

'Who has access to it?' Isabella asked sharply.

For a moment Claude looked worried. 'No one except myself, Monsieur Webster, Monsieur Fox and your father.' He trailed off and raked a hand through the white hair. 'To be truthful, Mademoiselle Isabella, I am grateful to be able to discuss this with you. Before he left Tom asked me not to discuss the break-in with anyone until he had sorted out the problem. Then unfortunately he had a heart attack.' The man shrugged his shoulders. 'It left me in a very precarious predicament. I did not know what to say when Monsieur Webster asked me why Tom had changed security.'

Isabella's eyes widened anxiously. 'What did you say?'

Claude threw up his hands. 'What could I say, *mademoiselle*? I had promised your father I wouldn't mention it to anyone, so I had to lie and say it was just that we needed a more modern system.' The man looked at her with deeply troubled eyes. 'I felt terrible, as I was sure that Monsieur Webster should have been informed of the truth. Probably your father was taken ill just before he could speak with him.'

'He was.' Isabella nodded her head slowly. 'But you did the right thing in not mentioning it to Monsieur Webster,' she assured him hastily.

The Frenchman frowned. 'But surely you don't think—?'

'I don't know what to think just yet,' Isabella cut across him crisply before he could voice her doubts. 'The fact remains that only Brady, Richard, my father and you had keys to that safe. So until I can get to the bottom of this mystery I suggest we keep the problem to ourselves.'

Claude was obviously uncomfortable with her suggestion. 'But I would think all the men who had keys to the safe were completely above suspicion,' he said flatly as he went to sit behind his desk. 'Especially myself,' he added as a small joke.

Isabella gave a small smile. 'Could anyone have got hold of your key?'

'No one.' The man waved her towards the seat opposite to him. 'I carry them on my person at all times.'

Isabella looked the man directly in the eye. 'Was either Richard or Brady around at the time of the break-in?'

Claude drummed his fingers on the polished wood of his desk, then opened the drawer beside him. 'Both had been visiting the factory the day before.' He took out a diary and flicked over the pages. 'Yes, the twenty-fifth of last month, both were here. Richard flew back to London the following morning, Brady to Switzerland. I discovered the files had been tampered with later that afternoon. But I don't think that either man would do such a thing,' Claude finished quickly.

'It doesn't look too good, though,' Isabella said drily. 'So, as I said earlier, I would prefer you not to mention any of this to either man until I've got to the bottom of it.'

But just how was she to get to the bottom of it? she wondered later as she sat back at her father's desk. She found herself remembering the letters Brady had received from Wolf-Chem this morning; letters marked urgent, yet he had not opened them at the table. She would dearly like to know what had been in them.

Maybe Brady was innocent? The thought stole into her mind. But then that only left Richard, and she couldn't see what reason he would have to try and steal the ideas for the perfume. No, Brady was the one who was working with a rival company, a company who just happened to be developing a new perfume… It was questionable, she thought grimly. The suspicions were ugly and distasteful, but Isabella couldn't stop playing with them.

The door to the office opened and the subject of her thoughts strode in at that moment.

He flicked a glance over the now tidy desk, the neatly stacked reports. 'You've done well,' he remarked, a note of surprise in his tone. 'I thought you might have needed my help with some of this.'

'I know it comes as a shock, Brady, but I am capable of dealing with elementary office work,' she replied drily.

'Hmm…that tinpot company in Paris must have taught you something after all,' he drawled with a hint of amusement in his deep tone.

'Verrell was not a tinpot company,' Isabella told him in no uncertain tone. 'For your information, it is a very highly respected company in Paris.'

'Such loyalty,' Brady murmured sardonically.

Isabella looked up at him sharply. 'There is nothing wrong with loyalty to your company, Brady,' she told him pointedly, perhaps a little too pointedly, but he didn't rise to the bait.

'I didn't say there was, Belle. But don't forget that you have supposedly switched allegiance to Brook Mollinar now.' He picked up her light jacket from the hook behind the door and threw it towards her. 'Come on, time for dinner.'

Isabella resented his attitude. 'I am not ready to leave yet,' she snapped as she picked up her jacket from the desk and put it behind her on the chair.

'Yes, you are.' Brady bent and pulled the plug out of her computer. 'It's six o'clock and I for one am starving.'

'Has anyone ever told you that you are completely overbearing?' she enquired furiously.

'No.' He flicked off her desk light and flashed her a smile that could only be described as wicked. 'People... especially women...usually like to do as I tell them.'

'And you are a chauvinist,' Isabella muttered angrily.

'Come on, you can tell me what else you like about me over dinner.' He grinned, not one bit put out by her comments.

'Our conversation is going to be very short at that rate,' she answered drily as she bent to pick up her bag.

'Where's Gemma?' Isabella asked as they made their way out of the building into the late afternoon sun.

'Claude is dropping her back to the house, seeing as we're going straight into Cannes to eat.'

'I would rather have gone back to the house first myself,' Isabella remarked. 'I would much prefer to shower and change before eating.'

'You look fine.' Brady opened the passenger door of his Mercedes for her, then marched around to the driver's side.

'Thanks, I'll try not to let the compliment go to my head,' she muttered sarcastically.

He grinned as he started up the engine. 'You are an extremely beautiful young woman, Belle, but I'm sure you already know that.'

Isabella's cheeks flooded with colour. She hadn't been fishing for compliments; in fact she would much rather he said nothing on a personal level to her at all. She cursed herself for her ready tongue. Sometimes she tended to say exactly what was going through her mind without thinking... It was a very bad habit and a dangerous one around a man like Brady.

'I'd rather you kept your observations to yourself,

Brady,' she told him stiffly. 'And to be honest with you I can't think why on earth we're dining out alone. I would have preferred to eat back at the house with Gemma.'

'I'm sure Gemma would be honoured to know that,' Brady said with a smile. 'But actually she is going out herself tonight, and as it's Madame Dupont's night off I thought a trip into Cannes would be most appropriate.'

'Oh, I see.' Isabella now felt foolish. Of course it was more appropriate that they went out. Staying alone at the house with him would have made her feel very awkward. Obviously Brady was of the same opinion. She glanced out at the passing scenery and lapsed into silence.

The sun was setting over the shimmer of the blue sea as they drove into the old quarter of Cannes and found a parking place. Isabella glanced down over the harbour and out towards the two small islands that were a few miles off shore as she waited for Brady to lock the car. 'It is still as beautiful as ever,' she murmured, breathing in the salty tang of the air.

'Yes, it's one of my favourite places.' Brady came around and placed a guiding hand at her back as they made their way along the narrow street. 'That's one of the reasons that I've just bought a boat. I often relax at the weekends down here, or sail down to St-Tropez or Cap-Ferrat.'

'Sounds wonderful,' Isabella said dreamily.

'Mmm…I think so. I feel I need to unwind after a hectic week of sitting in boardrooms and offices and travelling between London and Switzerland. It's good to get out into the fresh sea air, blow the cobwebs away, forget the pressures of business for a while.'

Isabella found herself wondering about the specific nature of his business worries. Did Brady have financial troubles? If so, it would be one reason why he might have delved into Claude's notes. If Wolf-Chem offered enough incentive, who knew what a desperate man might be driven to?

Brady opened the door of a quaint little bistro with bright red awnings, which looked out over the bay. Inside the place was humming with activity; even though it was still early, the place seemed full.

'We have a reservation for two.' Brady spoke to the *maître d'* and they were shown immediately to a secluded table in the corner.

'It's popular in here,' Isabella remarked as she reached for the menu.

'Yes, the food is excellent, especially the fish. It's brought in fresh from the harbour each day.'

'In that case I'll have fish.' Isabella studied the menu and chose shrimps *provenal* followed by sole and asparagus in white wine. Brady ordered *moules marinière* followed by lobster.

Brady was actually a charming dinner companion. She had forgotten just how entertaining he could be. He made her laugh, he made her relax, he made her forget that she wasn't supposed to like him. It was only when she glanced across and caught herself thinking about how attractive he was that the warning bells sounded.

'Would you like a dessert, Belle?' He glanced across and caught her watching him.

She shook her head quietly and reached for her glass of wine. Why hadn't he married Roberta? she found herself wondering, just as she had wondered many times over the years. Was the woman still in his life? She wouldn't have dreamed of asking; to do so would be stirring up all kinds of memories in his mind as well as her own.

'We will have the bill, please,' Brady told the waiter.

Isabella was a little surprised; she had thought that they would linger longer over a coffee. She didn't say anything, though. Maybe it was better if they made their way back to the house. The wine and the relaxed atmosphere had put her in a very strange mood.

It seemed to have got cooler outside now and Isabella was glad of the warmth of her jacket. They walked in silence down towards the car, but as they reached it Brady caught hold of her arm. 'I thought we would have a coffee and cognac on my boat before returning,' he said lightly.

Isabella looked up at him, wondering if she should refuse the invitation. Then she shrugged; what harm was there in sitting on a little boat drinking coffee? She allowed him to lead on.

There was a tranquil beauty about a harbour at night. Silver moonlight danced over the dark silky water. Boats bobbed up and down, making little lapping sounds as they pulled gently against their moorings.

There were some fabulous boats in the harbour. Large yachts from all over the world moored side by side, they spoke of incredible wealth and luxury. Isabella walked past them, looking for the small boat Brady had spoken of. She was stunned when he came to a halt outside one of the most magnificent power boats in the marina.

The *Sequester* was enormous. Isabella didn't know much about boats, but at a guess she would have said it was an eight-berth vessel. Giant masts pointed up into the star-spangled sky; the decks were polished timber. In reverence to its beauty Isabella took off her high heels before stepping across the gangplank and down on to the deck.

'This is fabulous, Brady,' she whispered as she looked around. She didn't know why she was whispering; maybe it was the silence of the night or maybe she was totally awed by the beauty of her surroundings.

Brady grinned. 'Thank you, Belle. It's my new toy.' He also whispered, a teasing light in his eyes. 'It's all right to talk out loud; you won't be ordered to walk the plank or anything.' He turned and led the way below deck.

Lights flooded the luxurious interior as he flicked a switch. They were in a large lounge area; blue settees were placed either side of a coffee-table. A crystal vase of blue irises complementing the décor sat on the highly polished surface.

'Please sit down.' Brady waved her to a seat and went to pour them both a brandy from the decanter on the bar area. 'I'll show you around in a moment.' He handed her her glass and then disappeared into the galley to switch on the coffee.

Isabella settled back against the soft cushions and her eyes moved over the pleasing décor. Obviously no expense had been spared with the boat. It made her theory that Brady might be in financial trouble rather laughable.

Brady returned with a tray carrying a coffee-pot and two china cups. He put them down on the table and then sat next to her on the settee.

'Do you think you are going to like working at Brook Mollinar?' he asked casually as he poured her a coffee.

'I think so.'

'You had some good ideas to put forward at your first board meeting.'

'Thank you,' she answered politely and took the cup and saucer from his outstretched hand. She felt uncomfortable when he paid her compliments like that. It made it hard to remember that he was someone she didn't trust, someone whom she must at all costs keep her distance from.

'Do you think you will miss Paris?' he asked, nonchalantly leaning back against the cushions and turning to look at her more fully.

'I loved living in Paris, but I don't suppose I'm going to get the time to miss it.' She sipped her coffee and tried very hard not to feel intimidated by his closeness.

'And what about your boyfriend? Do you miss him?'

The quietly asked question took her very much by surprise. Blue eyes flickered over to the dark, handsome man as she sought a suitable reply. 'I suppose I do,' she said carefully. 'I'm still in contact with Julien and I'll probably get to see him when he next has some free time from work.'

'That kind of relationship plays hell with a romance,' Brady stated drily. 'I'd say its days are numbered.'

That remark made Isabella angry. What did he know about her and Julien? 'I don't think so,' she said stiffly.

'Don't you?' One dark eyebrow rose. 'What does this…Julien do for a living?'

'He's a doctor at a hospital in Paris,' Isabella answered him after a slight hesitation. She didn't want to talk about Julien; her personal life was none of Brady's damn business.

'I'd say it's odds-on that now you are not around to keep his bed warm he will have found some attractive nurse to step in and replace you,' Brady said in a matter-of-fact tone.

Isabella's face went a bright shade of crimson at that remark. 'I don't think you should judge everyone by your own standards, Brady,' she snapped furiously.

He shrugged, not one bit put out. 'Sorry, sweetheart, but, like it or not, the fact remains that most relationships wouldn't survive the distance that's between you.'

'Well, thanks for the cynical lecture, Brady, but I don't think I needed it.' Isabella finished her coffee and put the cup and saucer back down on the table.

'Maybe not,' he continued, not deterred by her attitude at all. 'Maybe your boyfriend will give up his job and come to work at a hospital in London just to be near you.'

'I don't think that is very likely,' Isabella muttered almost to herself, and then promptly regretted the admission as Brady continued on briskly.

'Well, then, I'd say that there isn't a lot of future for you and your doctor.'

'Oh, for heaven's sake!' Isabella snapped, thoroughly fed up with the conversation. 'I really don't think my relationship with Julien is any of your damn business.'

'Probably not.' He finished his coffee and reached for his glass of brandy. 'I just wouldn't like to see you hurt. I know you're pretty keen on the guy; your father has kept me informed on that much. But quite frankly I can't see much of a future for you.'

Isabella blazed with anger. How dared he talk so intimately about her life...? As if he cared about her being hurt. The man had an arrogant nerve.

'Are you hoping to marry him?' he asked now, in the same casual tone.

'Maybe.' Isabella's voice was brittle with suppressed anger. 'As I said before, it's none of your business.'

'I suppose that's my cue to shut up.' He shrugged, unperturbed. 'Come on, drink your brandy, and I'll show you around.'

Isabella picked up her glass. She didn't particularly want to see around the boat now. The relaxed mood of the evening was gone, replaced by an angry tension inside her. How dared Brady make comments like that about Julien? She wouldn't have dreamt of asking about Roberta, even if she was filled with curiosity to know what had happened to the woman.

'Perhaps you would like to come for a sail at the weekend?' Brady asked idly now. 'I'm going to St-Tropez.'

'No, thank you.' Isabella rejected the invitation swiftly. The thought of being cooped up alone for a whole day with Brady was totally unnerving.

He shrugged. 'It was just a thought. Gemma said she would like to come and I wondered if you'd care to join us, get a bit of sunbathing done on the deck.'

'Oh…I see.' If Gemma was with them it might not be so bad; in fact it sounded very pleasant. She was half tempted to tell him she had changed her mind and would come, but he finished his brandy and stood up, and the moment passed.

'If you're ready I'll give you a quick tour and we'll head home.'

Isabella had never seen anything like Brady's boat. It was spectacular. The galley was fitted out with the most up-to-date equipment, rivalling any modern kitchen in a large house. And the cabins were the last word in luxury, especially the master bedroom. It contained a large double bed, a bathroom *en suite*, fitted furniture in the most beautiful carved mahogany and even a small study that led off it. Isabella found herself really regretting the decision not to join Brady and Gemma at the weekend. It would have been marvellous fun sailing down the coast. But her pride wouldn't allow her to tell Brady she had changed her mind.

They went back up on the deck. The night was bright with stars and there was the muted sound of music coming from a yacht further down the harbour. Isabella leaned against the rail of the boat and stared down into the swirling darkness of the water as she waited for Brady to switch everything off and lock up. The breeze carried a snatch of music clearly to her ears for a while. It was Nat King Cole singing 'Unforgettable', a moody love-song that Isabella had always liked.

Brady joined her and his hand rested against her waist for a moment. 'Lovely song,' he murmured. 'Very romantic.'

'I suppose so,' Isabella answered casually. 'If you believe in that kind of thing.'

'What kind of thing?' He turned to look at her, a gleam of amusement in his deep voice.

'A man finding a woman unforgettable.' The breeze blew a stray lock of blonde hair across her face and she brushed it away with an impatient hand.

'Oh, come on, Belle, I think you're a romantic on the quiet,' he drawled softly.

She shrugged, feeling slightly uncomfortable with the conversation. 'Maybe a little, but I'm also a realist. As you said earlier, it doesn't take long for a man to forget a woman and move on to pastures new.'

'Ah,' he murmured softly and tipped her chin up with a gentle hand to look at her more closely. 'Did I upset you by saying that?'

'No, of course not.' She jerked her head away from the touch of his hand; it made shivers race through her.

'I'm sorry if I did,' he carried on as if she hadn't spoken. 'It certainly wasn't my intention. Anyway, in retrospect maybe I was wrong. In most men's lives there is one woman who is unforgettable. Even if you don't end up with her, she'll haunt your dreams with what might have been...' He trailed off and then smiled wistfully at her. 'Come on, enough of this. Let's get back.'

He took her hand to guide her over the gangplank and they then walked in silence towards the car. Brady's words played and replayed in Isabella's mind. Had he been talking about himself? she wondered. Perhaps he didn't see Roberta at all now; perhaps she had finished with him and he really regretted losing her.

'Are you cold, Belle?' Brady asked as he noticed how she shivered suddenly.

'A little,' she murmured, yet it wasn't from the little breeze that played over the water. Her coldness seemed to stem from somewhere deep inside.

'Here.' He took off his lightweight jacket and passed it over to her. It was a chivalrous gesture and somehow it touched her in a kind of poignant way. Maybe Brady wasn't as awful as she had painted him over the years; maybe she was being most unfair to him in her character assessment.

'Thanks, Brady.' She took the coat and wrapped it around her shoulders. She could smell the faint lingering traces of his cologne from it. Strange how smell could stimulate powerful memories. The scent made her remember quite fiercely the pleasure of being held in his arms. The memory was so vivid for a moment that she could feel her face burning with heat.

'You OK?' He flicked her a glance as they came to a standstill next to the car.

'Fine.' Her voice was a trifle unsteady, and it was such a relief to hand that coat back to him.

'No, it's all right. Keep it until you're warm.' He opened the car door for her and she got in, her heart pounding uncomfortably. What on earth was the matter with her? she thought angrily as she watched him walk around to get in beside her. It wasn't as if she had any feelings left for the man. Why should she burn up with that incredible heat at the mere thought of his body close to hers? Must be embarrassment, she told herself rationally.

The powerful car gobbled up the miles along the coast towards Brady's house. Silence stretched between them and Isabella searched around for something casual to say to him.

'Where is Gemma this evening?' she asked finally.

'Out on a date.' He flicked her a glance from the twisty narrow road and seemed to hesitate for a moment before continuing. 'Some man she met when she was here last month. Obviously he found her unforgettable, because he rang her at the factory today.' There was an underlying hint of sarcasm in his deep voice.

'Oh...' Isabella didn't know what else to say. There had

been an idea at the back of her mind that Brady was romantically involved with his secretary, but obviously not.

The lights were on in the house as they pulled up the drive towards it. 'Looks as if Gemma has beaten us home,' Brady murmured.

Isabella couldn't help feeling relieved. It was a strain being alone with Brady and she had had enough for one evening.

Gemma was in the lounge with the man who had taken her out; Noël Marsaud was French and extremely handsome and charming.

'Hope you don't mind me coming in for a drink, sir,' he said as he shook Brady's hand.

'Not at all; make yourself at home. And the name is Brady.' Brady walked across and poured himself a coffee from the pot on the table. 'Isabella?' He glanced enquiringly over at her and she nodded her head.

'So where have you two been tonight?' he asked as he came to hand Isabella her drink.

'The new bistro in St-Tropez,' Gemma answered him with a smile. 'It was lovely; I can certainly recommend it.'

'Maybe when we go sailing at the weekend we can eat there in the evening,' Brady suggested as he sat next to her on the settee.

'That would be nice.' Gemma smiled in what Isabella thought was a very flirtatious way at her boss. Brady wasn't completely immune to her charms either, Isabella noticed, as he winked one dark eye at her in a teasing manner.

'See how I look after you? Not only are you having time to sunbathe this trip, but you are also getting to sail down the coast.'

'Sounds too good to be true; I'm sure there is a catch

hidden somewhere.' Gemma laughed. 'Are you sure you're not going to ask me to organise your office on board?'

'Well, come to mention it...' Brady trailed off and grinned teasingly. 'That might not be a bad idea.'

Gemma smiled and shook her head in a despairing manner. 'I might have known.' She smiled at Noël. 'My boss is a tyrant.' She spoke the words lightly, a laughing glint in her eyes.

'Well, as long as he keeps bringing you back to France,' Noël answered with a shrug, 'I'll think he's a very nice person.' He finished his drink and stood up. 'I think I should be going, *chérie*; I have an early business meeting tomorrow.'

Gemma also stood up. She was wearing a white dress that clung to her slender figure and then flared out just below the hips; it was extremely stylish and suited her to perfection. It was no wonder that Noël was so attracted to her, Isabella thought as she watched the other man's eyes following her every movement. Brady was also watching her, Isabella noticed.

'You are welcome to join us at the weekend if you like, Noël,' he said as the man turned to say goodbye to him.

'That's very kind of you. I'll try and arrange some time off and ring you on that, Gemma.'

'Fine.' She smiled politely at the man, but Isabella wondered if she wasn't a little disappointed that she wasn't going to be spending the time solely with Brady.

Noël turned and wished Isabella goodnight and then the two of them walked out as Gemma saw him to the door.

'Nice guy,' Isabella remarked lightly as they were left alone.

'Yes.' Brady's voice was dry and clipped.

Isabella finished her coffee and put the china cup and saucer down on the table next to her. 'Where did they meet?'

'He came up to the offices to ask if we needed any advertising and ended up taking Gemma out.' For some reason Brady's reply seemed somewhat guarded, and his eyes flicked towards the door as if waiting for Gemma to return. Was he jealous? Isabella wondered.

Gemma returned and sat back down beside Brady. 'It was nice of you to invite Noël,' she said, reaching for her glass. 'He was thrilled. I just hope if he comes that he doesn't spend all his time trying to persuade you to use his agency.'

'Oh, I think I can handle that,' Brady said easily. 'Anyway, I think that young man has other things on his mind when he's around you.'

Gemma laughed and glanced up at Brady with a coy expression. 'Do you think so?'

'Most definitely.'

'If you will excuse me, I think I'll turn in for the evening.' Isabella stood up. She felt tired, and on edge, probably due to the long day and the travel yesterday.

Brady also stood up politely. 'All right, Belle, see you in the morning.'

As Isabella left the room Brady went over and refilled Gemma's glass. Obviously neither was ready to retire for the night.

She found herself wondering again if there was anything going on between them. They seemed to have such a close working relationship and obviously Gemma was attracted to him, yet she had gone out with Noël and Brady had invited the other man on their outing. She couldn't work out the situation at all.

As she walked along the landing upstairs she noticed the door to Brady's bedroom was ajar and the light was on. She stopped for a moment and glanced in, wondering if she should turn it off.

It was a very opulent-looking room: dark blue satin

covers on the large double bed, white carpets and white fitted wardrobes, with double doors leading to an *en suite* bathroom. Isabella's glance, however, was drawn to Brady's briefcase, which was sitting next to the bedside table, a pool of light from the crystal lamp highlighting it. Was the briefcase locked? she wondered.

Generally, Isabella was not the type of person who would have dreamt of going into someone else's room, but the thought of the briefcase was extremely tempting. If it wasn't locked, then she would have access to the letters Brady had received this morning from Wolf-Chem.

She bit down on the softness of her lips, torn with indecision. The thought of reading someone else's mail was abhorrent, yet these were not normal circumstances. Those letters could hold the answer to whether Brady was responsible for the breach of security. A lot of money and indeed the future success of the company depended on her finding out who had gone through Claude's notes. She took a few tentative steps into the room.

Her heart was pounding nervously as she reached the bedside table and reached for the case. Her fingers had just closed around the handle when a cool voice behind her made her whirl around in panic.

'What are you doing in here, Belle?' Brady was standing in the doorway, the dark eyes narrowed and intent on her pale face. He looked stern; the handsome features were etched with disapproval, and Isabella swallowed anxiously, her mind whirling in a desperate attempt to come up with some plausible excuse.

'Sorry, Brady, but the bedside light was on and I came in to switch it off for you.' The explanation was lame even to Isabella's ears. The fact that she had been caught with her hands actually on his briefcase did not bode well. 'You should really put your briefcase out of sight, Brady,' she told him crisply now, somehow managing to look him in the eye as she spoke. 'I was just going to put it in the wardrobe for you. Anyone could walk in and probe around in it.'

One dark eyebrow lifted. 'Indeed, but I think they might find it disappointing; there is nothing of interest in there.' He moved into the room and across towards her. 'Your concern surprises me.'

'Does it?' Isabella tried very hard not to sound as nervous as she felt. 'Well, it shouldn't. I have a vested interest in anything that concerns the company. I wouldn't like just anybody to be able to read important documents concerning our business.'

'By "just anybody", who are you referring to?' he asked drily. 'Gemma or Madame Dupont...? Or maybe you think Noël has been up here?'

Isabella wasn't sure if he was being serious or not; she shrugged to cover her embarrassment. 'One never knows,' she said lightly. She would have walked past him and out of the room at that point, but he caught hold of her arm as she came closer, stopping her abruptly in her tracks.

'Not so fast. I think you should tell me more,' he said, and there was a note in his voice that sounded warning bells inside Isabella.

'More about what?' She looked up at him, a puzzled light in her eyes.

'Whatever it is you know,' he grated harshly. 'I hardly think you would come in here to move my briefcase unless you had some definite reasons to feel suspicious about these people.'

'Don't be ridiculous...I have nothing definite. I just think it's prudent to be careful.' Her voice held a slight catch, betraying her nerves.

'In that case I'd say you have a very weak excuse for coming into my bedroom,' he drawled lazily, but the grim tone had disappeared now, replaced by one of amusement.

His hand moved to her chin and he tipped her head so that she was forced to look him in the eye. 'Was there any other reason for you coming in here?'

'What other reason could I possibly have?' The question and the hand holding her made her tremble inside.

'I don't know of any, except the age-old one,' he drawled sardonically.

'The age-old one…?' For a moment she was genuinely perplexed.

'The one that is usually behind a woman's visit to a man's bedroom.' He looked genuinely amused as her face filled with colour at the implications. 'Is that what you wanted, Belle?'

Heat flooded her entire body. She had been so frightened of him guessing the real reason for her being here that she hadn't for one minute considered that he might think she was…was in some way after him. That he should imagine that she still carried a torch for him after all these years made her rigid with embarrassment and anger. 'Certainly not…' The words were spluttered out. 'That is the most ridiculous statement—'

'Is it, Belle?' he asked, his dark eyes never leaving her face. 'I seem to remember that you were once very attracted to me.'

'Of all the conceited—' The words started to burst out in an angry flood, but before she could get very far Brady had bent his head and his lips were on hers without any warning whatsoever.

She was so stunned that for a moment she just stood there while his mouth explored hers in a hungry yet strangely tender kiss.

'You didn't need to make up elaborate excuses, Belle,' he murmured softly against her lips. 'You only needed to ask.'

CHAPTER FIVE

'STOP, Brady.' She put a hand up against the silk of his shirt and tried to push him away. She was trembling violently, whether it was from shock or humiliation she didn't know. All she could think about was getting out of this room.

He took hold of her hand as it rested against his chest. 'You're shaking,' he murmured.

'Let go of me.' Her voice rose, an edge of her panic showing in it.

He released her immediately. 'Come on, Belle, don't get so upset.'

'Upset?' She stepped back and stared up at him with eyes that shimmered with anger. 'I might have been a naïve fool once, Brady, but that was a long time ago. Don't make the mistake of thinking that I'm the same person.'

'I never thought of you as a fool, Belle,' he murmured gently.

Isabella was not about to be taken in by that tone. 'You may as well save your smooth repartee and use it on someone a little more vulnerable, Brady. That is the way you like them, isn't it...young and naïve?'

The firm mouth slanted in a half-smile. 'I like them a little more mature these days.'

Isabella stared at him, unsure if that was some kind of a dig or an honest observation. 'Just keep away from me.'

'Perhaps if you kept out of my bedroom, honey, it would help,' he remarked sardonically. 'The way you're talking, anyone would think I was the one who had come to your room.'

Isabella's cheeks lit up with colour. 'I told you what I was doing. How was I to know that you are still so insufferably vain that you would think I was running after you?'

He seemed to find that remark amusing. 'I don't think you have any room to talk about vanity. As I recall, the eighteen-year-old Belle was a very pretty young girl who wore glasses.' He reached out a hand and tipped her chin so that he could look closely into her eyes. 'Now she wears contact lenses; what is that if not vanity?'

Isabella pushed his hand away roughly. 'That is called convenience. I find wearing lenses much better for my eyes. Not that it is any of your business.'

He shrugged. 'I was just pointing out that we're all human, Belle.' His eyes moved over the smooth creamy skin and her long blonde hair, taking in everything about her in detail. 'We all have our little weaknesses,' he murmured gently.

For a moment she was held under some kind of a spell as their eyes met. Brady still had a certain power over her senses, she realised suddenly; she could still look at him and feel her heart thudding against her ribs and her breath catching in a sudden rush of pleasure. The knowledge was most disconcerting.

She shook her head slowly and backed away from him. 'Anyway, Brady, just keep away from me. I'm here to work and you won't be able to pack me off out of your way so easily this time.'

He laughed at that. The laughter followed her as she moved towards the door. 'You can stay in my way as long as you like, Belle. I'm in no rush to get rid of you just yet.'

Isabella slammed his bedroom door behind her with

more force than she had intended. The man was insufferable; that she still found him attractive was beyond belief.

Gemma was just coming along the corridor at that moment and she gave Isabella a very strange look as they passed.

'Goodnight, Gemma.' It took all of Isabella's strength to get her voice to work in a normal fashion. The other woman merely nodded.

Had she overheard her conversation with Brady? Isabella wondered morosely. She went back into her bedroom and went straight through to her bathroom to have a shower. She needed to relax; she felt as tense as a tightly coiled spring. What a nightmare, she thought dismally, and she was still no nearer to finding out if Brady was the one who had looked through Claude's notes.

She felt a little better once she had stepped under the forceful jet of hot water. Her mind ran back over the day; it hadn't been too bad. She had achieved a lot of work, tidying up loose ends that her father had left. Then dinner with Brady had been quite pleasant. Her lips curved in a smile as she remembered some of the amusing things he had said. He could be very funny and very charming when it suited him.

She stepped out of the shower and wrapped a towel around her slender figure. No, the day hadn't been too bad. It would have been almost enjoyable except for the fact that she was here for a very serious reason. That episode in Brady's room hadn't helped matters either. Her cheeks burned as she thought about it. That man had such a nerve; imagine daring to kiss her like that!

Her eyes moved to study her reflection in the bathroom mirror. In appearance she hadn't really changed very much from that eighteen-year-old who had had a crush on Brady. Her skin was still satin-smooth, still prone to blushing when he teased her too much. Brady had made it very clear

a long time ago that he found her unattractive; why then
had he flirted a little with her? Why had he kissed her like
that…as if he was testing out her response?

She pressed a hand against the softness of her lips, remembering the melting feeling inside when he had kissed
her. Nobody had ever kissed her the way Brady did; nobody had ever made her feel so emotional inside with just
the merest touch of his lips. She shivered and immediately
switched her mind away from that.

Brady was an arrogant swine, she told herself heatedly.
He had been delighted to find her in his room and had
been only too willing to kiss her and test her response to
him, because it would suit him very well to have such a
powerful member of the board under his influence. He was
probably hoping very much that she was as naïvely taken
with him now as she was at eighteen. Well, he could think
again, she told herself furiously. The sensible mature
Isabella didn't give one damn about Brady Webster; the
man was a rogue and somehow she would find a way to
prove it.

Unfortunately, as that week progressed, Isabella had to admit that finding any proof of Brady being in any way corrupt was almost a laughable idea. She found nothing that
suggested anything other than Brady being completely capable and very trustworthy.

All the staff at the factory obviously liked and respected
him; that much was very apparent from the first. Even
Claude, who knew the true nature of her suspicions, told
her quite bluntly that he in no way sus-pected Brady.

Isabella worked her way through most of the large files
that Brady kept in his office under the pretext of bringing
herself up to date completely with the business.

It was late on Friday afternoon when she finished reading the last file. It was no wonder that Brady hadn't ob-

jected to her going through them, she thought with a sigh. There was nothing in them to suggest that Brady was anything other than a first-class business man. In fact the information she had gleaned from them had given her an insight into a brain that was brilliantly sharp. She even had to go so far as to feel a grudging respect for the man.

'Damn.' Her voice sounded loud in the silence of her empty office. She felt totally exasperated; a whole week had passed, and all she had proved was that Brady was an exceptional businessman, hardly what she had hoped for. Meanwhile time was passing and she was no nearer to discovering who had gone through Claude's files.

The phone rang on her desk and she snapped it up. 'Yes?' Her voice was crisp and businesslike.

'Isabella, there is a call for you from Paris; shall I put you through?' her secretary asked. 'It's a Dr Julien Arnault.'

'Julien!' Isabella's voice lifted with pleasure. 'Yes, put him through.'

'Hello, *chérie*.' Julien's voice was warm and very attractive.

Isabella smiled. 'This is a lovely surprise, Julien.'

'I rang your home and your mother gave me this number. I hope I'm not disturbing you?' he asked politely.

'Certainly not, it's a pleasure to hear from you.' Isabella was a little surprised at Julien phoning. He hadn't been pleased by her decision to go home to England, and their relationship had been left on rather a cool note.

'I received your letter,' he said now. 'And of course I'm not still angry with you. I understand that you had to leave Paris because of your father.'

'I'm glad.' Isabella rested her head back against her chair. 'I hated us to part on bad terms, Julien. I hope very much that we are still friends.'

'But of course, Isabella. You know how I feel about you.'

There was a moment's awkward silence. Isabella wasn't sure how she should reply to that. Julien had asked her to marry him when he had heard she was leaving Paris. The proposal had come as a complete shock to Isabella. Although she was very fond of Julien she had always just looked on him as a friend…nothing deeper than that.

'Imagine you being in France again so soon!' Julien carried on crisply. 'You might at least have phoned me; I could maybe have got down for the weekend.'

There was a tap at Isabella's office door and Brady strolled in at that moment, putting Isabella completely off stride with her conversation.

'That would have been nice, Julien,' she answered vaguely. 'But unfortunately I'm a little tied-up here at the moment. Once I've sorted everything out we will arrange something.'

She watched Brady perching himself on the edge of her desk and flicking idly through the files she had just finished with. His closeness was unnerving, as was the sardonic glance he threw her when he realised who she was speaking to.

'But surely you have some free time over the weekend, Isabella?' Julien persisted.

'Not really. Look, Julien, I have to go. I'll ring you back after the weekend and we'll talk properly.'

'Very well.' He sounded hurt now and Isabella felt guilty for fobbing him off so brusquely.

'I'll ring you very soon.' She dropped her voice to a more intimate level and tried to ignore Brady's presence.

'You promise? We need to talk, *chérie*,' Julien said now. 'It is very important to me.'

'Yes, I promise.' Isabella replaced the receiver, feeling very uncomfortable. She hoped Julien hadn't read more into that letter she'd sent him than she had intended. She really wanted to keep things just on a friendship basis between them. Perhaps she should have pointed that out once more while they were talking. She glanced up and met Brady's eyes.

'Is he missing you?' he asked drily.

Isabella shrugged. She didn't want to discuss Julien with Brady; it was none of his damn business.

'Well, I have some good news for you anyway,' Brady carried on. 'Elizabeth has just been on the phone; they are letting your father out of hospital today.'

'Thank heavens for that.' Isabella's relief was immense and a smile lit up her features.

'At least it's brightened you up,' Brady remarked with a wry twist of his lips. 'That's the first time I've got a smile out of you all week.'

'Well, I've been busy.' Isabella avoided his glance and started to tidy away the notes in front of her. She knew she had been cool towards Brady since that kiss in his bedroom. She wanted to keep her barriers firmly up when he was around.

'Yes, so I noticed,' he said with a sardonic note in his voice. He toyed with the file that she had just finished with. 'Find anything of interest?' he asked idly.

She glanced up at him sharply. Was that just a casual question or was there a deeper meaning behind it? she wondered. 'Not really,' she answered casually. 'Did you think I would?'

'Not really, but I suppose it was a good exercise for you. At least you're completely up to date with the production side of things.'

'Yes.' Isabella opened up her briefcase and dropped in the bundle of notes she had taken. 'How come my mother phoned you and not me?' she asked, changing the subject completely away from work. If Brady was responsible for the security breach, then she didn't want to alert him that she suspected anything. A change of subject seemed in order.

'She couldn't get through. You must have been on the phone with your French lover,' he said drolly.

She tried to ignore that remark; if he was deliberately trying to embarrass her he was doing a good job. 'She couldn't have tried very hard; I was only on to Julien for a few minutes,' she said abrasively.

'Well, I think she was in a hurry to go and pick Tom up. She asked if you would ring later on this evening.'

Isabella nodded. She had made a point of ringing home at six o'clock every day to find out how things were. It would be such a relief to ring tonight and know her father was home at last.

'Are you finished here?' Brady got up from the desk and glanced down at her with brooding dark eyes. For a moment she wondered if there was something bothering him, something he wanted to say.

'Yes, I am. Did you want something?'

'Only to get out of here and get some fresh air.'

'Oh.' She finished putting away the rest of her things. Obviously she had imagined that look on Brady's face. There was nothing bothering him other than overwork.

'I don't know about you, but I can sometimes feel the walls closing in on me at the end of the week,' he carried on.

'I suppose that's when you take off to sea,' she said lightly.

'There's nothing like it, Belle,' he murmured almost to himself. 'Heading out to open sea with the wind on your back...it's pure freedom.'

She had to smile at the wistful words. 'And then a storm blows up and that wind at your back becomes a hurricane,' she laughed. 'I think I prefer my freedom on dry land, thank you.'

He smiled and reached to ruffle her blonde hair with a playful hand. 'But that's life, isn't it, Belle? One moment smooth waters, the next a raging storm. It's the unexpected around every corner that makes for excitement.' For a moment he considered her with a more serious look on his face. 'You used to be the type of girl who liked excitement. You always rose to a challenge, a sparkle of determination in those beautiful eyes.'

Isabella's heart thudded uncomfortably at the sudden swing in the conversation. 'I don't know about that.' She stood up and reached for her briefcase, trying to call a halt to the discussion.

'Don't you?' He caught hold of her hand for a brief moment. 'There was a time when you were frightened of nothing; now…' He paused, searching for the right words. 'Now you are guarded, as if someone or something has knocked that sparkle out of you.'

Isabella pulled her hand away from his. 'That is just nonsense, Brady,' she told him crisply. 'I'm no different from how I was. And I'm certainly not afraid of anything.' She avoided his eyes as she spoke, because there was a little part of her that knew what he was saying was right. She was more guarded these days… She was afraid, and she knew with a sudden clarity just why that was. She was actually afraid of him, scared to death to allow herself to drop her barriers around him in case he succeeded in making a fool out of her again.

She swallowed hard. 'Now I thought you said that you were ready to leave?'

'I'm ready whenever you are,' he said with a shrug. He stood and watched as she walked around the desk, her head held high, yet an unconsciously vulnerable light in her eyes.

'So will you be coming out on the boat with us this weekend?' he asked in a conversational tone as they went out into the corridor and waited for the lift.

'No, Brady.' She still didn't dare to look at him. 'I've already told you I will not be coming.'

The lift doors opened and they both stepped in. 'Why not?' he persisted. 'I thought you said you were not afraid of anything.'

'I'm not. I've just got a lot of work to get through while I'm here.' There was a tinge of annoyance in her voice. She just wished that he would leave her alone.

'Well, if I can make some spare time, I'm sure you can.' The doors opened and they walked out across the cool marble hall and then through the automatic doors to the car park. A blast of hot air greeted them as they stepped into the sunshine. 'What work is it you have to get through? Maybe I can help.'

'No, thank you, Brady. I don't want your help.' Isabella sounded thoroughly annoyed now.

'Well, there's no need to snap, Belle,' he said drily. 'I was just trying to be friendly.' He opened the car door for her and she got in, feeling guilty now. There had been no need to speak to him in that tone.

'Sorry.' She glanced across as he got behind the driving-wheel.

'I'll forgive you.' He smiled, a teasing light in his eyes. 'But only if you say you'll come sailing tomorrow.'

'Really, Brady!' She turned to look out of her window with exasperation. Did the man never give up?

'I promise to check the weather reports before we set off,' he said sardonically now, 'so you have nothing to be afraid of.'

Isabella wasn't so sure about that. It wasn't the weather she was bothered about. She shrugged slim shoulders. 'All right, then, you've convinced me,' she said haltingly.

Maybe it wouldn't be too bad, she told herself. After all Gemma and her boyfriend were also coming, so it wasn't as if she would be alone with Brady.

'By the way, where's Gemma?' Isabella turned to ask him with a frown.

'Noël is picking her up and they're going into Cannes for dinner.' Brady started up the engine of the car.

'But they're still coming sailing tomorrow?' Isabella asked anxiously.

'I don't know.' Brady shrugged. 'Probably,' he said with a smile. 'But, then again, they might prefer to be on their own.'

They travelled home in silence after that. Isabella was wishing with all of her heart that she hadn't weakened to his invitation. If only she had stuck to her guns and said she didn't want to go. Now she faced the prospect of being alone with him all day tomorrow, and it made her nerves go into overdrive.

He pulled the car up the sweeping drive towards his house and it dawned on her suddenly that not only would they be alone tomorrow, but tonight also, as Gemma was out.

Brady parked the car outside the garage and they walked up to the front door. The sun was setting now and the day was losing some of the intense heat. The sprinkling system in the garden started up and there was a sweet smell of lavender and roses in the air.

'It's a beautiful evening,' Isabella murmured softly as she looked down over the velvet green lawns and the colourful flowerbeds.

'Yes; unfortunately I don't think I'm going to see much of it.' Brady put his key in the door and it swung open. 'I've got a lot of work to get through this evening. If you don't mind, Belle, I think I'll take a working dinner and just stay in my study this evening.'

'I don't mind at all,' Isabella said lightly, trying not to sound too relieved.

'Good. Well, Madame Dupont will no doubt keep you company.' Brady put his briefcase down on the hall table and picked up a pile of mail that had arrived for him by the afternoon post.

Isabella could tell his mind was miles away as he spoke. It was obvious he was still thinking about business. She wondered vaguely if he was preoccupied with Brook Mollinar business, or Wolf-Chem?

Isabella hardly slept a wink that night. She tossed and turned and worried constantly about the next day's outing.

It was totally ridiculous, she told herself as she got up that morning. Imagine being so worked up just because she might be left alone with Brady! She was a grown woman now and well able to deal with Brady Webster; nothing would happen. After all, the two of them had been left alone last night and she had had no problems.

She went through to have a shower and then came back to study her wardrobe. What should she wear? After a good deal of indecision she selected a pair of white shorts and a navy and white cropped T-shirt. She had only brought one brief bikini, which she had thrown into her case at the last moment, thinking that she probably wouldn't have time for sunbathing anyway. As she looked at it now she wished that she had brought something a little less revealing. Still, it was the only thing she had, so it was going to have to do.

She put the bikini on underneath her clothes and then studied her reflection in the long-length mirror. Her golden hair was sitting perfectly in long silken waves; she looked tall and slender in the shorts. She would do, she thought nervously. Then, throwing a towel and some sun cream into a bag, and also a skirt and cardigan for the evening, she went downstairs in search of Brady.

He was in the conservatory finishing a cup of coffee and studying the morning papers. Isabella had never seen him look so relaxed. He was wearing blue shorts and a white short-sleeved shirt that emphasised the powerful arms and the dark, healthy tan of his skin.

'Good morning.' As soon as she appeared in the doorway he put down the paper and reached for the coffee-pot. 'What can I tempt you to? Croissants? Crusty rolls? Or would you like toast?' Brady indicated the food on the table next to him.

'Croissants would be lovely.' Isabella sat opposite to him in the matching wicker chair and tried not to notice the way his eyes moved over the long length of her legs.

'Is Gemma not down yet?' She picked up her coffee-cup and glanced across at him.

'She didn't get in until one o'clock this morning, so I don't think she's able to face getting up at this early hour. I said we would meet her and Noël for lunch out at Sainte-Marguerite, one of the Lérins islands off the coast of Cannes. They can get a ferry out and join us.'

'Oh, I see.' At least she would only be alone with Brady for the morning, she thought thankfully. It could have been worse.

They drove into Cannes along the coast road. The sun was starting to rise high in the sky now and it promised to be another scorching hot day. The Corniche was a most spectacular stretch of road, hugging the side of the cliffs and giving dazzling views out across the sea towards hidden bays and little villages nestling along the shores. Isabella relaxed back into the comfortable seat and enjoyed the scenery and the drive. She was glad that Brady was such a competent driver, as the road was quite narrow in places and it wound around hairpin bends with startling drops down towards the Mediterranean.

'This reminds me of the day I picked you up from Nice airport when you came to stay with me for the summer,' Brady remarked casually.

The comment made a tingle of awareness shoot through Isabella's body, and immediately her relaxed mood was gone. She didn't want to talk about her previous visit here; it stirred up far too many emotions.

'Does it? I can't say I remember too much about that.' She turned her head away from the sharp glance he shot towards her.

'You can't remember?' He sounded very amused, and it was no wonder, Isabella thought bitterly. It was extremely unlikely that she would ever forget that summer. She had arrived in France young and innocent, her heart full of dreams. Brady had shattered those dreams, taken the naïve young girl and turned her into a woman. She was hardly likely to forget such a momentous summer, the summer she had grown up.

'Well, I suppose a lot of things have happened since then,' he murmured as she did not answer him. 'You passed your exams at university, you lived in Paris, and of course you met your doctor boyfriend.'

'Yes.' Isabella stared straight ahead, her face composed into a cool, inscrutable mask.

'Do you think you will marry him?'

The quietly asked question cracked her composure for a moment and she turned startled eyes on him. 'Really, Brady, you ask the most impertinent questions,' she muttered angrily. 'I've told you before that it is none of your damn business. I don't go around asking you such personal details.'

'Fire away,' he said sardonically. 'I have no secrets.'

She frowned. 'There is nothing I would like to know,'

she said stiffly. It was a lie, of course. There were a million things she would like to ask Brady, such as what had happened to Roberta…and did he break into Claude's files? But she wouldn't have dared to voice those questions, and anyway, even if she did she probably wouldn't get a truthful answer.

The car turned a bend in the road and Isabella could see Cannes stretched out in front of them. The long palm-fringed promenade with the golden sandy beach had never looked so welcoming, she thought gratefully. Perhaps now that they were nearly at the boat Brady would change his conversation and she could forget everything but the sun and the beauty around her.

They drove into the old quarter of the town in silence and only when Brady had parked the car did he resume the conversation, and then only briefly. 'So you have not one shred of curiosity where I am concerned,' he said with a strange expression in those deep, dark eyes.

'Not one shred.' She reached for the door-handle and got out. Why didn't he just let the conversation drop? she wondered angrily.

'I'm disappointed.' He locked the car and walked around to join her. 'I thought we were still friends.'

She glared at him. Why did he always succeed in making her feel as if she was being unnecessarily churlish? 'We are business associates,' she said brusquely.

'Ah, I see,' he drawled with a tinge of sarcasm. 'And of course business associates cannot be friends.'

Isabella decided it was time to draw a complete halt to the subject, so she didn't rise to the bait. 'What time did you say we were meeting Gemma and Noël?' she asked instead, looking up at him with wide eyes.

'You know I said we were meeting them for lunch,' he said with a wry twist of his lips. 'Don't panic, Belle, you're not going to be stuck with me for long.'

'I wasn't panicking.' She followed him down towards the boat.

'No?' He turned to give her a helping hand to get on board the luxury vessel. There was a mocking light in his dark eyes, made even worse by the fact that she ignored his outstretched hand and walked on board unaided.

'No.' She flicked her blonde hair in an almost defiant manner as she passed him. 'I know you like to cultivate this idea that I'm overawed by you, Brady, but I can assure you that is not the case. I do not feel in any way intimidated by you.' Liar, a little voice whispered inside her as she turned to look at him. He was watching her with a look of amusement on his lean, handsome features.

'Glad to hear it.' He turned and started to busy himself with getting the boat ready for leaving port. 'In that case you can make yourself at home. Take one of the sunloungers out on deck and relax.'

It wasn't long before they were gliding out over the smooth waters of the harbour. Isabella sat on the lounger, enjoying the heat of the sun and the spectacular views out over the bay. The old town with its steeply rising streets and the Suquet church at the top was slowly left behind as they headed for open water.

'You OK?' Brady looked over at her for a brief moment.

She shaded her hands over her eyes to look up at him against the sun. 'Fine.'

'Haven't you brought some sunglasses?'

'I forgot to put them in my bag,' she admitted reluctantly.

'I have a spare pair down in my cabin; go and get them if you want.' His eyes moved over her slender figure. 'And put on your swimming-costume if you want to do some serious sunbathing.'

'I'm all right, thank you,' she said self-consciously. 'But I will borrow your glasses, if you don't mind.'

'Of course I don't mind.' He turned his attention back to the controls of the boat and she went down below deck to look for his cabin.

It was cool down there after the intense heat of the sun. She walked down the narrow corridor and looked through each doorway. Brady's cabin was the largest. A double bed dominated the room, and beside it on the table was a pair of Ray-Ban glasses. She picked them up and turned to leave. On the way out she noticed the door leading off to his small office was open. For a moment she hesitated and then went to have a closer look.

A desk with a computer and fax machine stood in one corner and the complete wall behind it was taken up with filing-cabinets. Isabella moved further into the room and glanced at the papers that were sitting on top of the desk.

There wasn't much of interest there; it was mainly personal correspondence. She was just leaving when a red folder caught her eye. It was marked 'Private', but it was lying half open, as if Brady had been working on it then had to leave in a hurry, forgetting to lock it away. She reached out a slender hand and pulled it a little further open. It was marked with the Wolf-Chem stamp and there was something about perfume written in red letters underneath. She pulled it closer, her heart pounding.

'Have you found them, Belle?' Brady's voice calling down the passage made her jump, and she moved very hurriedly away from the desk and out of the room before Brady could come down.

'Yes, I have them.' She met him just on his way to look for her. 'They were where you said.' Her voice sounded breathless. She felt nervous; it was silly, but Brady was so astute that she felt he knew she had been snooping.

'Good.' He gave her a strange look as she brushed quickly past him and went back up on deck. 'Everything all right?' he asked, following her up.

'Wonderful.' Gratefully she put on his dark glasses. The boat was anchored a little way off shore from the island of Ste-Marguerite, she noticed now.

'Do you want to go ashore for a while or would you prefer to do some sunbathing on here?'

'May as well go ashore.' She looked out at the island, but her mind was not on the scenery now. Her brain was wondering what had been in that file and if it would connect him in any way to Claude's notes.

'OK, we'll take the small dinghy in. The waters around here aren't deep enough to sail in to.'

She nodded but said nothing.

'Are you sure you're all right?' he asked after he had lowered the boat, and came over to give her a hand getting down into it.

'Yes, Brady.' Her voice was abrasive. 'Don't keep asking me that.'

'Sorry, sweetheart.' He started up the engine and then turned to grin at her. 'You just looked a little pale and I was worried that the heat might be making you feel ill.'

Did he have to be so pleasant? Isabella thought angrily as the boat sped across the water towards the island. There was something about Brady that made it almost impossible to remain aloof from him. He could be so utterly charming, so caring.

The breeze blew Isabella's blonde hair into wild disorder around her face, and she pushed it back with an impatient hand. 'I like the heat, Brady,' she said, trying very hard to sound polite. 'It rarely makes me ill.'

'All the same, don't forget to put plenty of cream on. You have a beautiful skin; you don't want to burn it.'

Isabella bit down on her lip. When Brady threw a compliment at her like that it made her feel most uneasy. Her heart thumped like something crazy and she felt as if she had been running some kind of a race, she was so breathless.

The boat slowed and Brady manoeuvred it into the island with superb skill. He smiled at her as he reached to help her out. 'Unless you want to get your feet wet I think I had better carry you ashore.'

'I don't mind getting my feet wet.' She angled her chin upwards in a determined manner as he shook his head laughingly.

'OK, off you go.'

He watched as she took her shoes off and slipped over the side of the boat. The water was deeper than she thought. It came up over her knees and if a sudden wave caught her she was in danger of getting her shorts wet.

Brady also got out of the boat, but the water only came over his calves. He had lovely legs, she noticed idly. Strong and deeply tanned. She stumbled and nearly ended up swimming ashore.

'Here.' Impatiently Brady caught hold of her and before she could complain he had swung her up into powerful arms and was carrying her ashore. Her heart pumped unmercifully against her chest at his closeness. She prayed that he didn't notice just how flustered she was just at being held by him.

He put her down on the shore and grinned at her. 'You see, I don't bite...even if you are a rather tasty morsel.'

Before she had a chance to formulate a reply to such a disconcerting sentence he was heading back through the water to bring the boat closer in.

Isabella sat down on a piece of driftwood as she waited for him to come back. The island was silent and hot; the only sound was the call of the birds. She looked about her with interest; the coast was a little rocky at this point. Behind her there were thick woods. There was a tranquil atmosphere that was very restful to her ruffled nerves. The scent of eucalyptus and pine lingered in the salt air.

'Ready.' Brady splashed back through the water and reached out a hand to help her stand up.

'This place looks very beautiful,' she remarked as they followed a little path around the coastline.

'Yes. It's the larger of the two islands, about two miles long, and beautifully kept, very unspoilt.' Brady caught her arm and pointed out across the sea. 'That is St-Honorat island. It's named after St Honorat, who withdrew there in the fourth century to found a monastery. As the island was out of bounds to women his sister Marguerite founded a religious community on this island—hence its name.'

They carried on walking. Brady did not release his hold on her arm as they came to a rocky bit of the path. 'The story goes that St Honorat would only allow his sister to visit him on his island once a year, when the almond trees were in bloom. Marguerite promptly planted an almond tree and prayed so hard for a chance to see her brother more often that it began to bloom once a month.'

Isabella smiled. 'She sounds as if she was a very determined lady.'

'Yes. St Honorat saw in the miracle the sign of divine intention, and allowed her to come to visit whenever she wanted.'

'That's a lovely story, Brady,' Isabella murmured. 'It certainly says something for the power of prayer.'

'Yes.' Brady veered off the track. 'Come on, we've just got time to look at the old fortress where they once held the man in the iron mask prisoner.'

Isabella thoroughly enjoyed exploring the island. As well as being a place of extreme beauty, it was steeped in history. Brady was a good guide; he seemed to know all the relevant facts about everything.

'It's a hobby of mine,' he said later as they sat at an

outdoor restaurant with a panoramic view across the sea towards the hustle and bustle of Cannes. 'I enjoy reading history books, especially about places that I have a special love for.'

'I don't know when you get the time to read,' Isabella said lightly.

'Oh, you'd be surprised. I do have some lonely evenings to fill sometimes.' He said the words with a gleam of dry humour.

'I don't believe that for a moment,' Isabella remarked, looking away from him and out at the cornflower-blue of the sea. Brady Webster was far too attractive ever to have a lonely moment. 'I'd say you'd only have to flick your little finger and you'd have a flock of women running to your side.' She hadn't meant to say anything so personal; it somehow just slipped out.

'Maybe,' he murmured. 'But I don't particularly want a flock of women. Just the right one.' His voice was gentle and somehow tinged with regret.

She glanced across at him, surprise clear in her wide eyes. He was probably joking, yet he looked so serious. His dark eyes met hers steadily. Was he talking about Roberta? she wondered suddenly. Perhaps he had really loved her. Why hadn't he married her? she wondered for the hundredth time.

'What happened to Roberta, Brady?' Curiosity overtook all her strong resolve not to pry. Immediately the question left her lips she regretted it.

His firm lips curved in a smile of genuine amusement and there was certainly no regret in those deep eyes now. 'Why, Belle,' he drawled in a mocking tone, 'I thought you had absolutely no interest in me whatsoever?'

'I don't,' she snapped crossly. 'I just thought you sounded a bit wistful.'

'Did you, now?' he drawled. 'And don't tell me that

you care, Belle.' The dark eyes raked over her delicate features and she could feel herself colouring up with embarrassment.

'I was just making polite conversation.' She looked away from him. 'Just forget it,' she told him crossly.

Brady didn't get a chance to say anything else on the subject, because at that moment Gemma and Noël arrived.

'Hope we're not too late for lunch?' Gemma asked brightly as they picked their way across the terrace towards them.

'Certainly not. We just had a drink while we were waiting for you.' Brady stood up politely and pulled out the chair next to him for her.

Gemma sank down into it gratefully. She looked stunning in a short skirt that flared out over her slender hips and a matching top in a pale ice-cream shade of pink. 'I don't think I've found my sea legs yet,' she admitted ruefully. 'That short sail over in the ferry from Cannes has made me feel a bit shaky.'

'You get seasick?' Brady asked with surprise.

The woman nodded. 'I'm afraid so. It's years since I went sailing. I thought I'd be better than I used to be, but...' She trailed off and shrugged her shoulders regretfully. 'I'm afraid I'm not.'

Noël sat down next to Isabella and smiled at her. 'The poor girl has been looking more than a little green,' he told them.

'Now don't exaggerate.' Gemma glared over at him. 'I wasn't that bad.'

The waiter arrived and handed them all a menu. 'Maybe you shouldn't sail with us to St-Tropez, Gemma,' Brady said as the waiter left them again. 'It's not worth it if you feel ill.'

Gemma looked very disappointed at that. 'No, I'll be fine...honestly,' she reiterated as he continued to look at her in disbelief. 'I've taken a travel-sick pill, so I should be all right now.'

'All the same, I would choose a light lunch if I were you,' Brady recommended as they all studied the menus.

Both women chose a *salade niçoise* while the men had steaks. It was a delightful lunch, sitting looking out over the sea. Cannes was a distant hive of activity. As much as Isabella liked the town, it was relaxing to be away from it. The sun beat down from an azure-blue sky on the tranquil little island, and Isabella found herself understanding the need for retreat. How lovely it was to be away from the hustle and bustle of traffic, to sit and hear nothing except the swish of the water and the cry of the birds and only the occasional snatch of someone else's voice.

Isabella drank a couple of glasses of wine, something she rarely did in the afternoon, and for a while she felt as if she were here on holiday and forgot the awful suspicions she had about Brady Webster.

After a very leisurely couple of hours they made their way back to the boat. There was a great deal of laughing as Noël tried to pick Gemma up to carry her to the small dinghy and stumbled in the water, nearly dropping her.

When they got back on the boat Isabella made coffee in the galley. She carried the tray up to the upper deck, where Gemma was stretched out on a lounger in a brief yellow bikini bottom and nothing else. The men were both up at the controls of the boat, talking.

'Coffee,' Isabella called out to the men and set the tray down on the table before sitting down on one of the other loungers.

She had thought that Gemma would put her top on once the men came down to join them, but on the contrary, the woman sat up and adjusted her sun-bed but made no move to cover up.

'This is the life,' she said with a grin as she reached for her coffee. 'I wish all our business trips were this pleasant.'

'I can't spoil you too much, Gemma.' Brady came and sat down on the opposite lounger. 'It goes against the grain. You know I'm really a slave-driver at heart.'

Gemma laughed. 'Well, I can see you've got Noël organised.' She nodded her head up to where the other man was still busy on the bridge.

'I'm just trying to impress him, so he'll offer me a job,' Noël laughed. 'I've always liked the idea of being a deck hand. It beats advertising, I can tell you.' He came to sit down and reached for his coffee.

'That reminds me, Noël. Call up at my office on Monday morning and we'll discuss those ideas you have on an advertising campaign for the company,' Brady said crisply.

Noël nodded. 'Thank you, Brady. I do have one or two new ideas for you.'

Isabella glanced over at the man. Was it her imagination or was there a slight edge to his tone?

Noël grinned at her. 'I just didn't like to mention work today in case Brady thought I was taking advantage of the relaxed, friendly situation.'

'You should always take advantage of a relaxed situation,' Brady told him with a grin. 'I can assure you the best deals are struck that way.'

Isabella leaned her head back against the lounger and closed her eyes against the heat of the sun. Obviously it was her imagination; the two men seemed perfectly at ease.

Had Brady taken advantage of a relaxed situation at Brook Mollinar? she found herself wondering suddenly. She wished she could get to the bottom of that particular problem; it was starting to eat away at her. She opened her eyes and looked across at Brady.

He was leaning indolently back against the soft cushions of his lounger, his dark eyes narrowed as he looked out to sea. He was so incredibly attractive, she thought with a catch of her breath. If only she could have trusted him...if only—

'You'll get lines if you continue to sunbathe dressed like that,' Gemma interrupted her thoughts. The other woman was sitting rubbing oil liberally into her body. She gleamed in the sun, smoothly golden and firmly curving in all the right places.

Isabella wondered if she was deliberately trying to be provocative. Noël was certainly watching her with great interest as he lounged back in the sun. Brady on the other hand had got up and was heading for the controls of the boat as he got it under way towards St-Tropez.

Isabella took off her shorts and top and reached for her sun cream. She wasn't about to take off her bikini top. It wasn't that she was a prude, but she couldn't possibly have relaxed lying half naked with Brady about. Anyway, she thought as she applied the cream and lay down, her bikini was brief enough.

The sun was hot and the soothing lap of the water against the boat lulled Isabella as she lay looking up at the clear blue sky. The next moment, she had fallen asleep.

A gentle hand on her shoulder brought her awake. She gazed up sleepily, straight into Brady's dark eyes.

'I think you've slept long enough, sweetheart,' he said gently.

Isabella swept a hand through her blonde hair and sat up. They were alone and the boat was anchored in a picturesque little harbour. Pink and white houses lined the waterfront. Brilliant colours reflected in the water lapping against the quay. People strolled along the front looking at the expensive boutiques or just sat at the pavement cafés.

'Where are we?' she asked muzzily.

'St-Tropez.' He grinned. 'You've been asleep for a couple of hours.'

'Have I?' It was probably due to the lack of sleep the night before. She stretched and then noticed how his eyes followed the movement of her slender body in the very brief bikini. Immediately she reached for her T-shirt. 'Where are Gemma and Noël?'

'Gone home about fifteen minutes ago.'

'You should have woken me.' Isabella put on her T-shirt and glared at him. 'I would have gone back with them.'

'I don't think Noël would have been too pleased. He had other plans, I'd say.' Brady smiled at her. 'Anyway, I thought you would be staying to keep me company tonight.'

'I beg your pardon?' She stared at him blankly.

'Well, I plan to stay here overnight—go out for a meal to that new bistro that Gemma recommended and then sail back to Cannes in the morning.'

'You mean you want me to stay overnight?' She couldn't help the outraged tone. The idea shocked her completely.

'That was the idea.' His dark eyes gleamed with amusement. 'Don't look so panic-stricken, honey. I hadn't planned to ravish you.'

She was furious at such a comment. 'I don't give a damn what you have planned,' she said staunchly. 'I have no intention of staying here.'

'Why not?' He reached out a hand and ruffled her blonde hair. 'Don't be such a coward,' he said mockingly. 'Besides, there is something important that I would like to discuss with you.'

She sat up, her interest aroused. 'What's that?'

'I'll tell you later.' He got up and grinned down at her.

'You can have the cabin next door to mine. How does that sound?'

It sounded dreadful. Warning bells were ringing in a persistent niggling sound right through her entire system. 'I don't know, Brady... I didn't bring any overnight things.'

'That's all right. Your bathroom is well equipped with anything you might need. As for a nightdress...' He trailed off, a teasing gleam in his eyes. 'I'm sure you won't need one of those.'

Isabella wasn't sure how to reply to that, so she remained silent. He took her silence as acquiescence and smiled. 'Right, make yourself at home. Go and have a shower if you want.'

Isabella glared at his receding back as he walked away. This was a big mistake, she just knew it was.

CHAPTER SIX

THE intense heat of the sun was fading as Isabella and
Brady got off the boat and strolled along the promenade.
The *Sequester* was moored alongside some fabulous
yachts. They bobbed up and down in the late afternoon
sun, adding a certain glamour to what once had been just
a small fishing village.

Artists stood with their easels, painting the colourful
harbour. Isabella stopped now and then to look at their
work. One in particular had captured the beauty of his
surroundings perfectly. Colour vibrated from his canvas
just as it did from the walls of the buildings along the front.

Brady stood behind her as she admired it and praised
the artist on his work.

'How much will you sell it for?' he asked the man in
his fluent French.

The artist shrugged. 'It is not finished, *Monsieur*.
Tonight I will work some more on it and maybe tomorrow
it will be ready to sell.'

Brady nodded. 'We will come back tomorrow.'

'It's a lovely picture,' Isabella murmured as they moved
across the road.

'Yes, but then he does have a very good subject to work
on. St-Tropez is a very picturesque little spot.' He took
hold of her arm. 'Come on, I'll show you the view from
the top of the hill before we go and have dinner.'

They walked up a narrow side-street which wound
steeply upwards. At the top of the street a grassy hill

stretched farther up, dotted with wild flowers and trees. A little path led up towards what looked like a fort on the top. It was quite a walk and Isabella was glad they weren't making it in the full heat of the day. When they got to the top, however, she was so taken with the view that she had to admit it would be worth the walk even at midday.

The small village nestled below the green of the hill, the red-tiled roofs contrasting sharply with the sparkling blue sea. A round church tower jutted up above the rest of the roofs and its bell rang out joyfully, the sound carrying clearly in the sea air.

'It's so beautiful,' Isabella murmured, her eyes following a yacht that was sailing in towards the harbour, its white sails flapping in the gentle breeze.

'Out across the water is Port-Grimaud.' Brady pointed across the bay. 'That is also very lovely. It's like a miniature Venice and was built only a few decades ago on land reclaimed from the sea. I'll take you there one day; I'm sure you will like it.'

Isabella's eyes moved from the scenery towards him. 'I don't think we will have time to go on any more trips, Brady. I was planning on going back to London this week.'

Brady nodded. 'And I have an important meeting in Basle on Wednesday. I meant that I would take you there next time you come to stay.'

Isabella doubted that there would be a next time for staying at Brady's house. Being close to him was too much of a strain on her emotions. Even now, despite her mistrust of him, she still felt drawn to him, and deep down she was starting to hope that her suspicions were very wrong.

As she looked up into the darkness of his eyes she wondered for a moment if she was still a little in love with him. The idea sent a shiver of fear through her and she swallowed hard. No, she rejected the idea forcibly. She

couldn't have any feelings for a man she didn't trust. She
had learnt her lesson about Brady and learnt it well.

'Ready?' He held out a hand to help her down the hill.

She ignored it. 'I can manage, thank you,' she told him
and made her way down the path in front of him.

The bistro he brought her to was small and intimate and
very stylish. Isabella wished she had put on something a
little more dressy than her pale pink skirt and the matching
cotton top with a sweetheart neckline. She was unaware
of how her skin glowed with health from the day out in
the fresh air and how bright and luminously beautiful her
eyes were as Brady looked across the candlelit table at her.

He stretched across to pour her some wine. 'You were
a very lovely teenager, Belle, but you have grown into a
very beautiful young woman.'

The compliment startled her, but she managed to accept
it with a graceful smile. 'Thank you, Brady. And now that
we have enjoyed a bit of light-hearted frivolity perhaps we
could get down to discussing that bit of business you mentioned earlier?'

'Let's enjoy our dinner first,' he said crisply. 'How is
your steak?'

'Very nice.' She frowned at him. Why was he drawing
this out? If there was something important he wanted to
discuss, why didn't he just get on with it?

'How do you think your father will cope with retire-
ment?' he asked, and the question successfully distracted
her thoughts.

'I think he will find it difficult,' she answered slowly,
her mind turning towards her parents. 'You know what
he's like about the company, Brady. He's lived for it over
the last few years.'

'He can be proud of it, though. He took it from a small
business and made it into a huge success.'

Isabella nodded. The business had originally been in her

mother's family. The Mollinars had run it on a small scale, then Tom Brook had walked into their lives and he had transformed it radically. It was now international, with chic retail outlets in major cities and a most impressive headquarters in London.

'He is a man to be admired,' Brady reflected.

Isabella looked across at him. Did he really think that about her father? And, if so, would he really try to ruin what Tom had worked so hard to build? The idea suddenly seemed so unlikely that it was ludicrous. 'Brady, there is something I think you should know…' She blurted the words out, then came to an abrupt halt.

'Yes?' He was watching her with a serious light in his dark eyes, and suddenly she changed her mind. She shouldn't say anything about the breach in security until she had certain proof that he had nothing to do with it.

'Yes?' he prompted her again, a slight edge to his voice.

'Nothing.' She played with the food on her plate for a moment, then put down her cutlery. She had lost her appetite.

'It didn't sound like nothing,' he prompted, a gentle note in his deep tone.

She glanced across at him. At that moment she would have given anything to unload the problem on to him, would have given anything to be able to trust him.

'Belle?' He reached across and for a moment his hand touched hers as it lay on the table. The sensation made her tremble inside. 'If there is something troubling you, you only need to say, and I will sort it out for you.'

She swallowed hard at that, then shook her head. 'It's all right, Brady, it was nothing.' She reached for her wine glass and finished the drink. 'Actually, all that fresh air today has made me very tired.' She forced herself to meet his eyes again. 'If you wouldn't mind, I'd like to call it a night.'

'No, I don't mind.' He signalled for the waiter.

It was dark outside now but the promenade was lit with the bright lights from the restaurants and the boats. They walked in silence to the *Sequester*.

It was strange how much it felt like home here, Isabella thought as she walked back on deck.

'A nightcap?' Brady asked as he went to pour himself a glass of whisky.

Isabella nodded. 'I'd like cognac, if you have it.' She sat down in one of the comfortable armchairs. She was reluctant to retire to her room for some reason, even though at the back of her mind she knew that was what she should be doing.

He handed her the drink and sat opposite. There was silence for a moment except for the gentle lap of the water against the sides of the boat. A crystal lamp threw gentle light over his features. He looked deep in thought.

'Why did you ask me about Bobby this afternoon?' he asked suddenly.

Her hands tightened around the large glass. 'I told you, I was just curious.' She tried very hard to keep her voice light.

There was silence once more and Isabella thought for a moment that he wasn't going to say anything more on the subject.

'On the contrary, I thought that you had said you had no curiosity where I was concerned,' he said finally, a teasing light in his eyes for a moment.

She sipped her cognac. 'It was just a passing comment, Brady,' she replied idly.

'Well, in answer to your passing comment, yes, I do sometimes see Bobby,' he drawled lazily.

'I see.' It was strange how her mouth seemed to go dry at that knowledge, how her heart beat painfully against her chest.

'I don't think that you do,' he murmured. 'Bobby is one of the top directors at Wolf-Chem. It is inevitable that we bump into each other.'

Isabella studied the amber liquid in her crystal glass with an air of indifference to what he was saying, yet inside all her senses were tuned into the conversation. 'So you broke off your engagement to her?' She tried very hard to sound as if she were only expressing a casual interest.

'I was never engaged to Bobby,' he replied steadily.

Her eyes flew to his face in surprise. 'But she said that you were... She led me to believe that you had an understanding!'

'Did she?' He shrugged. 'We did see a lot of each other at one time, but it was never serious. At the risk of sounding conceited, I would have to say that marriage was a little bit of wishful thinking on her part.'

Apart from being stunned, there was a part of Isabella that felt a glimmer of happiness at this revelation, but she passed no comment; to do so would only have given him the idea that she cared. And she didn't care...did she? She glanced down at her drink and tried very hard not to analyse her feelings too deeply in case she didn't like what she found.

Brady downed the rest of his whisky. 'So now you know,' he said with a wry twist of his lips.

'Well, it's all in the past now,' she managed to say lightly.

'In the past, yes,' he said softly. 'But the past is not forgotten, is it, Belle?'

She glanced up sharply at that question and the dark eyes held hers in a way that made a shiver race down her spine.

'I...I don't know what you mean.' She looked away again hurriedly.

'I mean that I remember very clearly your youth and

beauty, the way you used to look at me with passion in those deep blue eyes.'

Isabella felt her breath catch in her throat at those words. She shook her head sharply to dispel the warmth that threatened to seep up under her skin. He was teasing her…testing her responses in some sort of game, and she wasn't going to fall for it. 'As you said, I was young…I was infatuated by you.' She forced herself to admit those words to him and then meet his eyes directly. 'But it didn't last long and it meant nothing.'

She could see that her words displeased him; there was a glimmer of anger in the dark eyes for a moment. 'You will have to forgive me, Belle,' he said smoothly, 'but for some reason I don't think those words ring true.'

She put her brandy glass down with a hand that wasn't entirely steady. 'Well, I can assure you that they do. That summer is long forgotten, Brady,' she told him in a husky tone.

One dark eyebrow lifted disdainfully, and there was now an arrogant light in his eyes, almost as if he might at any moment be able to prove in some way that she was lying. It was a ridiculous notion, but it made Isabella's every nerve-ending tingle with fear.

The shrill ring of the telephone interrupted them. He reached out for the receiver with an impatient hand.

'If you will excuse me, Brady, I think I'll turn in for the night.' Isabella got to her feet hastily, seeing this as a heaven-sent opportunity to escape the awkwardness of the conversation.

He nodded curtly and she turned away to go below deck. As she went down the stairs she heard him speaking in German in a brisk and efficient tone. He sounded annoyed. The door swung behind her and she could hear nothing further.

Her heart thudded in her breast as she walked down the

narrow corridor towards her room. She was so relieved to have escaped from that conversation that her legs actually felt weak beneath her.

It was hot in her cabin. She turned up the air-conditioning, took out her contact lenses, and then went for a shower in the *en suite* bathroom. As the forceful jet of water streamed over her body she tried very hard not to think any more about Brady, to close her mind to the evening's events, but it was nigh on impossible. Her conversation with him kept thundering through her mind again and again.

He had never been engaged to Roberta! That one startling fact burnt her very soul, and along with it was the memory of the way he had looked at her when she had told him that her infatuation with him was a thing of the past.

There was a man's silk dressing-gown hanging behind the door and she put it on. She noticed wryly that it had Brady's initials embroidered on the pocket in gold thread. It was far too big for her, but the silk felt cool against the heat of her skin and she kept it on and went back through to her room to lie on top of the bed and stare up at the darkness of the ceiling.

Despite the shower, sleep was evasive. Isabella was not relaxed; her mind was active. Over and over again she thought about the way Roberta had declared that Brady and she were engaged. Then she remembered how Brady had sent her away...the look of scorn on his hand-some features.

Why had he brought up the subject of her infatuation with him? Why was he taunting her so blatantly with it, when all she wanted to do was forget it? She turned and rested the burning heat of her cheeks against the coolness of the pillows as she remembered again what a fool she had felt that night so long ago when she'd whispered that she loved him.

The boat moved a little against its moorings as the wind got up. Isabella turned again restlessly and looked at her watch. Without her contact lenses the dial was fuzzy until she held it away from her. It was four in the morning already, and she hadn't slept a wink. She got up and, tying the belt of her dressing-gown more securely, she went to get herself a drink.

The narrow corridor was lit with just one light now; it was enough to be able to negotiate the steps up to the lounge and find her way across towards the galley. She found some orange juice in the fridge and, pouring it out, she moved on to the deck for a breath of fresh air.

The weather seemed to have changed. It was cool out-side now and a breeze was sweeping in across the sea. It whistled through the riggings of the boat in an eerie way, almost like an unearthly cry of a tormented soul. Isabella shivered and turned to head below deck again. She prac-tically collided with Brady.

His hands shot out to steady her and for a moment she was held close against the warmth of his body.

'Sorry.' She stepped back hurriedly.

His eyes moved over her slender body in the fine silk dressing-gown. 'You shouldn't be out here like that.' His voice held a note of censure. 'The temperatures have dropped and it's damn cold tonight.'

'There's no need to snap; I was just getting a breath of fresh air.' She side-stepped past him, noticing that he was still fully dressed.

He reached out a hand and caught hold of her arm. 'Sorry, honey,' he murmured in a deep, dulcet tone now. 'I didn't meant to sound annoyed; I guess I'm just tired.'

She hated it when he turned so charming; it made her want to melt inside. 'That's all right.' She pulled away from his hand and tried to just forget that their early conversation had taken place. 'How come you're not in bed?'

'That phone call was some urgent business I'll have to attend to tomorrow. I was getting a head start by doing some paperwork tonight.'

'You won't be fit to see to any urgent business tomorrow if you don't get some sleep,' she replied lightly.

He smiled a trifle drily. 'Why, Belle, you almost sound as if you care.'

Her skin coloured a delicate shade of red at that remark. 'I was just being practical, Brady.'

'Ah, was that all?' he whispered, a mocking tone in the softness of his voice. 'For a moment there you raised my hopes.'

Isabella glared at him. Why was he always so intent on making fun of her? 'Don't be so damned facetious,' she snapped in a low tone. 'And, as I've said before, I don't care; I don't give a damn, in fact.' Then she marched away from him. 'Damn man,' she muttered to herself as she started to go below deck. How was it that he was able to raise her blood-pressure with the utmost ease?

She wondered what business he was seeing to tomorrow and suddenly found herself remembering that he had been going to discuss some important business with her last night. With all the talk about Roberta and the past she had completely forgotten about that. Should she ask him about it now?

She glanced back towards him as she started to negotiate the step down towards the cabins. It was a mistake. The dressing-gown she was wearing was far too long for her and it caught under her foot. One moment she was at the top of the steps and the next she was at the bottom, lying in a crumpled heap on the floor.

Brady was beside her in a moment. 'Are you all right,

honey?' Gentle hands came to help her as she struggled to sit up.

'I think so.' She felt slightly dazed. Her back hurt where she had hit it on the stairs and her elbow was grazed and bleeding.

'Anything broken?' His hand moved to her leg, which was lying at a slightly twisted angle underneath her.

'No.' She moved sharply away from the touch of his fingers and then became aware that the dressing-gown was showing a little too much of her body than was modestly decent. The belt had loosened and one side had slipped down, showing a creamy expanse of her shoulder and breast. Hurriedly she pulled it straight; his eyes followed the movement and she felt herself blushing with embarrassment.

'Can you stand?' He put an arm around her and pulled her up to her feet.

She gingerly tried to put her weight down on her foot. It wasn't too bad; in fact the worst of the pain was from her back and her elbow. 'I'm all right, Brady,' she murmured. Then as his arm still continued to hold her she made a determined effort and pulled away from him. 'I'm fine…' She stumbled and put a hand on his shoulder. 'Really I am,' she muttered breathlessly.

'OK, come in here for a moment.' He led her down the corridor and swung the door beside him open.

Gingerly she moved past him, then stopped. He was leading her into his bedroom!

'Brady, this is your room.' She tried very hard not to sound panic-stricken.

'So it is.' He grinned. 'Come on, honey, I'm not going to bite you. I have a first-aid box in here. I'm just going to patch that elbow up for you.'

'I don't need—'

'Do as you're told for once, Belle.' He cut across her

impatiently and made for the cabinet in the *en suite* bathroom.

Making a face of displeasure, Isabella moved into the room. Whom did he think he was talking to? she wondered angrily.

She caught sight of herself in the gilt-framed mirror of the bathroom and forgot her annoyance for a moment. The pale silk of the dressing-gown was bright red with blood on the sleeve. 'On, no, Brady,' she groaned. 'Your lovely dressing-gown.'

'It will wash out,' he said matter-of-factly. 'Now let's have a look at your arm.' Before she had a chance to avoid him he had caught hold of her and was leading her towards the wash-basin.

She winced as the warm water ran over the broken skin. 'Gosh, that is sore.'

'Soon be better.' Brady gently bathed it and then, holding her arm firmly, he applied some antiseptic cream and a plaster.

'Thanks.' She moved away from him as soon as he had finished. She knew he was only trying to help, and he was being very kind, but his close attention made her heart beat a rapid tattoo against her breast.

'Now I think you should take off that dressing-gown and I'll throw it in the wash,' he said casually.

She glanced up at him, her eyes wide and startled, and he laughed.

'I'll get you a T-shirt or something else to wear. Don't worry.'

'I wasn't worrying, I was just—'

'You were just panicking like mad.' Brady finished her sentence for her with a wry grin. 'I'll get you one of my shirts.' He disappeared through to his room and pulled out the set of drawers by his bed to find a suitable top for her.

Isabella watched him silently from the bathroom. She

felt foolish. How stupid to fall down those steps! And now
she was standing like some spare part in his bathroom,
panicking because she didn't want to be in such close
proximity to the damn man.

'Here.' He tossed her a plain white shirt. 'I'll go and
get you a drink while you put it on.' He disappeared out
into the corridor.

Isabella didn't waste much time. She took off the dressing-gown and slipped on the shirt. It was far too big for
her and it showed an alarming length of her legs. She
surveyed her reflection in the bathroom mirror critically.
The white shirt looked like a mini-dress and it certainly
was far too revealing to be walking around in. Hurriedly
she bundled up the dressing-gown and moved through to
the bathroom. Her intention was to leave and return to her
own room immediately, but her attention was caught by
some paperwork sitting out on the bedside table and, distracted, she moved to have a closer look at it.

She flicked over the cover. Without her contact lenses
she couldn't read it very well, but it looked like the file
she had seen in Brady's study marked with the Wolf-Chem
logo. She sat down on the edge of the bed and held it
away from her as she strained her eyes to try and read it.
Some of it was in German, but there was some English.
She bit down on the softness of her lower lip in agitation.
If only she had put her contact lenses in. For all she knew
this could contain some evidence that would link Brady
with the breach of security at Brook Mollinar. She clicked
her tongue as she flicked over more of the pages.

'Perhaps I can be of help?' The dry voice from the doorway made her jump violently.

She looked up to see Brady leaning indolently against
the door-frame, a glass of brandy in his hand.

'I...I'm sorry, Brady. I didn't mean to be nosy.' She

swallowed hard and looked up at him with what she hoped were wide, innocent-looking eyes.

He smiled, but it was a smile singularly lacking in humour. 'If I recall rightly, this is the second time that I've found you snooping.'

'I wasn't snooping.' Her voice held an outraged tone. The word snooping made her sound as if she were some busybody.

'No? So what were you doing?' He came across and put the brandy down on the bedside table, before taking the file out of her hands.

'I...I was just glancing at the file while I waited for you. The thing is in German, Brady, and anyway I'm not wearing my contact lenses, so I could hardly be reading it, could I?'

'Maybe not.' His mouth twisted wryly. 'But, judging by the way you were holding it up, it's not for the want of trying.'

'What utter rubbish. I only glanced at the damn file.' Anxious to be away from him, she started to stand up, but he put a firm hand on her shoulder and pushed her back down.

'Not so fast, honey. You are not going anywhere until I get an explanation.'

'I've explained that I was just idling away some time while I was waiting for you.' Nerves made her voice rise sharply.

One dark eyebrow lifted. 'So let me get this straight... Last time I caught you trying to pry through my business papers you assured me that you were just putting them away out of harm's way and that being in my room had nothing to do with waiting for me.' His eyes moved over her scantily clad body, the long length of her bare legs. 'And this time...' he continued in a deep, honeyed tone.

'This time you are assuring me that you were waiting for me.'

Hot colour flooded her face. She didn't like what he was trying to imply; in fact her hands clenched into tight, nervous fists as she sought around for a suitable reply to such an outrageous suggestion. 'I'm saying no such thing.' She breathed the words in an agitated rush. 'You went to get me a drink...remember? I was waiting for it.'

He smiled and lifted the brandy glass and then caught hold of her tightly clenched hand to soothe it open and placed the cool crystal into her grasp. 'There you are, then.'

He still continued to stand so close that she couldn't move from the bed. Her hand shook slightly as she lifted the glass to her lips. She took one sip of the warming liquid and then put it down on the table again.

'So what are you waiting for now, Belle?' he asked steadily, his eyes never leaving the soft curves of her lips.

'I'm waiting for you to move out of my way so that I can go back to my own room.' She was so nervous now that her voice actually sounded hoarse.

'Do you know, sweetheart, I don't think that is what you're waiting for at all,' he murmured softly, his eyes moving over the tanned glow of her skin against his white shirt, the soft, luxuriant fall of her blonde hair around her shoulders. 'I think you're waiting for this.' Then he leaned closer and tipped her chin firmly up with one hand to place a kiss against the softness of her lips.

She moaned softly in protest beneath the pressure of his mouth, but he didn't release her; instead he deepened the kiss and his hand moved from her face down the side of her neck and towards her body. She could feel his hand touching her through the thin material of the shirt, caressing the soft curves of her breast with a hand that was firm yet so tender that it made Isabella's heart miss a beat and a wave of pure pleasure sweep through her.

His lips lifted and he looked down at her. Isabella wished with all her heart that she could see the expression on his face through clear eyes, but it was slightly hazy to her.

'Isabella?' The question in his voice was unmistakably clear.

She nodded her head and swallowed hard. This was a mistake; this was something she had vowed would never happen.

His hand moved to the top button of the white shirt and he started to undo them one at a time, very slowly.

It was up to her. She only had to stop him, put one hand over his, and he would stop, she knew that. She knew that Brady Webster was a lot of things: a rogue—albeit a charming one—a shrewd and cunning businessman, but he was not the type to force himself on her. It would be so easy to stop things now and yet at the same time it was impossible. Impossible because she didn't want him to stop. The knowledge hit her hard, like a train running out of control; one fact after another flew into her mind and raced around and around. She wanted Brady; she wanted him with all her heart.

The white shirt fell open. 'Yes, you are even more beautiful now than you were at eighteen.' Brady's voice was husky and sweet to her ears. 'And those blue eyes still look at me with searing heat.' His hand trailed a silky-soft caress down over her naked skin.

'Brady...' Her voice was a mere whisper; she was lost in a whirl of blinding passion.

CHAPTER SEVEN

THEIR bodies were entwined so closely that it was almost as if they were one. Arms were wrapped around arms, legs twisted around legs. Isabella's head was resting on Brady's chest. She could feel the steady beat of his heart, the deep rhythmic rise and fall of his body as he slept deeply.

Tentatively she moved so that she could look up at him. He stirred slightly as she rolled to one side and his grip around her shoulders tightened for a moment in an instinctively possessive way.

His features were slightly indistinct to her eyes. The strong lips were curved in a smile. He looked happy, she told herself and rested her head back against his chest.

Their lovemaking had been deeply passionate, it had blocked out everything in Isabella's mind except the wonder of being with the one and only man she had ever really loved. She admitted it freely to herself now and nuzzled her head in against him to brush her lips over the satin-smooth skin.

She had spent so many years trying to block him out of her mind, trying to tell herself that she hated him, despised him, and all along she had been lying to herself. She had realised that the moment she had allowed herself to surrender to him. The barriers that she had built up against him over the years had crumbled so easily that it had been frightening. She loved him now just as she had loved him at eighteen.

His hand moved around her waist, catching her in even

closer against the lean, powerful length of his body. She smiled softly to herself. 'Brady, I love you.' She whispered the words into the silence of the early morning. The words that she had whispered so many years ago. 'I've always loved you.'

Silence met her words. She raised her head slightly to look up at him; he was still asleep. She sighed and ran her hand idly over the soft whirls of hair on his chest. She would tell him when he woke up. She would tell him everything: her feelings for him, her worries about the business, everything.

It seemed so awful now the way she had distrusted him. Of course Brady wouldn't have had anything to do with a security breach at the factory. She had allowed personal feelings to cloud common sense; she just hoped that Brady would understand and forgive her. She bent her head and kissed the flat plane of his stomach. If he felt the same way about her as she did about him he would forgive her, she thought with a rush of confidence, and after the way he had made love to her last night he must have deep feelings for her. She kissed his skin again, loving the feel of his firm skin beneath her lips, the tangy, clean male smell of him.

'Keep doing that and I'm not going to make it to my business appointment today.' His velvet-deep voice shocked her.

He was awake! Had he heard her telling him that she loved him? Her heart pounded painfully as confidence receded into the silence of the morning. 'Why not let business wait today?' she whispered softly and snuggled up to kiss his neck.

'I wish I could,' he groaned and wound his hands through the silky softness of her hair as he lifted her head and his lips found hers. 'Last night was wonderful,' he murmured huskily against her mouth.

'Yes…' Her breath caught painfully in her throat; she couldn't find the words to tell him how wonderful.

The alarm buzzed insistently on the bedside table and Brady stretched out a hand to switch it off. 'I have to get up, sweetheart,' he said with a tone of deep regret. 'I have a meeting in Basle today.'

She swallowed hard. 'Yes…I understand.' She pulled the silk sheet closer around her naked body as she sat up a little self-consciously. Silly to feel so conscious of her body when he had explored every inch of it so thoroughly last night.

Brady jumped out of bed. Unlike her, he had no reservations about walking around naked. He had a superbly fit body, she thought as she watched him covertly from the bed. Lean and powerful and beautifully tanned.

He flicked a glance down at her and smiled. 'You look beautiful.' He leaned down and his lips found hers in a lingering warm kiss. His eyes wandered over the slender shoulders, the white silk sheet held tightly around her. 'I wish I didn't have to rush off like this, Belle,' he murmured gently. 'But I have a responsibility to the other shareholders at Wolf-Chem. There has been something of a power struggle within the company and our meeting has had to be brought forward to today. A lot is at stake at the moment and if I don't turn up a lot of money will be lost.'

She nodded; she did understand, but it was hard. She had spent so many years trying to forget him and now that her barriers were down and her emotions raw and open she needed to hear reassurance; she desperately needed to hear him say that he felt deeply about her. 'Brady.' She reached out to him as he made to move away.

'Yes?' His dark eyes were gentle on the soft curves of her face, the wide blue of her eyes.

'We need to talk; there are things I need to say,' she said hesitantly.

He nodded. 'Don't I know it. I've spent so long trying to forget you, Belle…' His words trailed off as she flung her arms around his shoulders.

'Oh, Brady.' Her heart pounded with relief; he did feel the same way. She looked up at him and her eyes misted with sudden tears.

'Hey!' He brushed a gentle hand under her eyes. 'You're not crying, are you?'

She shook her head, feeling foolish. 'I'm just so happy.'

He smiled. 'Come on, get up and we'll have breakfast together.'

She nodded and got up, conscious that his dark eyes were watching her with a gleam of pleasure. As she put on the white shirt that she had been wearing last night he turned away and picked up the phone from beside the bed.

'Gemma?' His deep voice sounded calm and relaxed, a million miles away from the way Isabella was feeling. Her emotions were leaping around like a Yo-Yo—first happiness, and then despair that Brady had to go.

'We have to leave for Geneva this morning. Pick me up from the boat, and we will head straight for the airport,' he ordered crisply. 'Oh, and Gemma, send my chauffeur down to pick Belle up…what? Yes, we're still at St-Tropez.'

Isabella left the room to return to her own bedroom, pressing down a feeling of resentment that Gemma was able to accompany Brady.

He was in the galley when she went up a little while later. 'Coffee?' He held up the pot and flicked an enquiring glance over her.

She had changed into the skirt and top she had worn last night. Her hair was still damp from the shower; her skin was slightly flushed. Feeling self-conscious, she just nodded. How was it she felt such a mess and he looked so…so devastatingly handsome? Her eyes moved over him shyly.

He was dressed for the office this morning. A dark business suit, a white shirt and silk tie accentuating the breadth of his shoulders. His dark hair was neat and crisply combed into place. It was hard to imagine that this incredible man was the same one who had made love to her with such wild abandonment last night.

'Croissants?' he asked with a grin. 'I don't know about you, but I've worked up quite an appetite.'

Her skin flared with even brighter colour. 'Just coffee would be fine.' She walked over and opened the cupboard beside him to get out a china cup and saucer. It was a relief to busy herself doing something. Her heart was pounding so loudly that she felt sure he would be able to hear it.

He took the china from her as she turned around, and put it on the counter beside him. 'Belle?' He tipped her chin so that she was forced to look up at him. It was surprising, the difference that wearing her contact lenses made. She thought she could see a slight coolness in his dark eyes now, a slight wariness. Was it her imagination? Was she just so unsure of herself, of their relationship, that she was searching for problems? Or had that edge been there even last night? Had last night just been a one-night thing for him?

Fear made cold hands clutch at her heart now and her blue eyes had a vulnerable light in them as they held his.

'Belle?' His hand moved to her back as he moved her firmly closer.

She winced slightly at the pressure of his hands, and he frowned.

'Belle, are you all right?'

She nodded. 'My back is a little sore after my fall, that's all.'

He looked relieved for a moment and her heart lifted.

'Will you wait for me at the house? I should be back some time tomorrow night.'

Her heart lifted even more and sang with sheer pleasure. She nodded. 'I'll wait.'

'Good.' He placed a firm kiss on her lips. 'I don't want you running off on me again.'

She refrained from saying that she had never run off. He had sent her away. She buried the thought in the far recesses of her mind and forced herself to smile. If she wasn't careful she would break down and abandon pride to the winds and demand to know his exact feelings for her. Their relationship was far too tentative at the moment for that. 'How about that coffee?' she forced herself to ask lightly.

He turned and poured them both a cup of the steaming liquid. 'Will you be all right on your own at the house?' he asked crisply over his shoulder. 'Madame Dupont will stay overnight if you ask her.'

'There's no need, I'll be fine.' Isabella swallowed hard. They were talking like strangers. If only he would utter some word of love.

He turned and handed her the drink. 'Let's sit down.'

They moved up into the lounge. The weather seemed to have changed during the night. The blue skies were slightly overcast. A breeze whistled around the boat.

Brady sat opposite to her, his eyes moving over her in a gentle way.

'Is there anything in particular you would like me to do at the factory while you're away?' she asked to cover the awkwardness of the silence between them.

He shook his head. 'I want you to rest.' He grinned in a rather wicked way. 'And I don't particularly want to talk business with you right now.'

'No...' She was out of her depth. There was so much

she did want to say to him. All those things that she had been so positive about in the warmth of his arms early this morning. Now, in the cool light of day, she was tongue-tied, frightened to make a fool of herself again, the way she had done so many years ago.

'Last night meant a lot, Belle.' He put his coffee down and leaned across to reach for her hand. 'I'd like to think that—'

Whatever he had been about to say was interrupted by the sudden arrival of Gemma. She tapped gently on the glass panel of the door and stepped inside. 'Gosh, it's a little cooler today. The mistral has blown in.' Her eyes noted the hand that Brady still had over Isabella's. 'Sorry, did I barge in on something?' There was a slight edge to her voice.

'No, that's all right.' Brady released Isabella and sat back. 'You were quick. Would you like a coffee before we leave?'

The other woman nodded and came and sat next to him on the settee. She looked stunningly attractive in a beige trouser-suit. Her blonde hair was sleekly groomed back off her face, her make-up impeccable.

'You had two phone calls last night, Isabella,' she said casually as she took the cup of black coffee from Brady. 'One was your mother. She said it wasn't important, she would ring you today. The other was someone called Julien. He said it was important and would you please phone him first thing this morning.' The woman sipped her coffee. 'I didn't give him the number here as Brady only likes very urgent messages to be put through and this did sound personal.'

Isabella nodded. 'That's all right. I'll phone him later.' She met Brady's dark eyes. They were cool and watchful. 'It's probably nothing.' She tried to sound dismissive.

'Do you think so?' Brady's voice held a slight dry edge. 'Does he usually use the word urgent about nothing?'

'Well…no…' She shrugged, not knowing quite what to say, especially in front of Gemma.

'Is Bernard here yet?' Brady changed the subject abruptly.

'He's outside,' Gemma answered and started to drink her coffee quickly. 'What time are we flying?'

'Ten o'clock. I thought we'd take my car to the airport. Bernard can take Belle home.'

Isabella presumed that that was her cue to leave. 'I'll just get my things,' she said stiffly and rose to her feet.

Her heart was pounding as she made her way down to her cabin. She felt as if she was being dismissed again, just as she had been when she was eighteen.

She flung the few things she had brought with her into her bag, then found herself thinking about the tender moments they had shared last night. Her emotions were well and truly shaken up. One minute she was furiously angry with Brady, the next she was melting inside as she thought about the way he had held her.

She took a deep, steadying breath. She was going to have to catch hold of her sensitive feelings and control them. Brady was in a hurry for a business appointment. The way he had made love to her showed how very much he cared about her, she told herself briskly. She glanced quickly around the room to make sure she had forgotten nothing, then she made her way back up to the lounge area.

Only Gemma sat on the settee now. 'He's out speaking to the chauffeur,' she said as Isabella glanced around for Brady. 'Sit down and finish your coffee.'

Isabella shook her head. 'I've had enough, thanks.' She put her bag down on the chair and crossed to the window to look out. Brady was indeed outside on the quayside, leaning indolently against a silver stretched limo as he talked to the driver.

'Making sure that Bernard is going to take you home safely,' Gemma said as she came to stand beside her and followed her eyes out towards Brady.

Isabella glanced around at the woman. There was a definite dry edge to that remark. Was she just a little bit jealous? 'You sound bothered?' she ventured in a tone of idle curiosity.

'Bothered?' The woman's eyes widened and then she laughed. 'Oh, you think that I'm romantically interested in my boss? I can assure you, Isabella, that I am not so foolish as to fall for Brady. No...' She shook her head and moved back to the settee to finish her coffee.

There was a moment's silence as Isabella waited for her to continue with a feeling of dread. She didn't really want to hear what the woman was saying, yet a brooding kind of curiosity made her listen on.

'I'm his personal secretary, remember? I'd say I know him better than any of his women friends. I'm the one who organises the sending of flowers, the little messages to tell them he is otherwise engaged in a business meeting when in fact he is out with another woman.' She laughed drily again. 'Oh, no, Isabella, as attractive as Brady is, I have much more intelligence than to fall for him. I know that he is ultimately a loner, a man who enjoys an affair but nothing more serious than that.' She put down her cup and saucer and turned her attention crisply to her gold wristwatch. 'Time is moving on. Brady will be waiting for you.'

'Yes.' Numbly Isabella reached for her handbag.

The woman was jealous, she told herself as she stepped out into the crisp morning air. It was nothing more than that. But doubts were already set where Brady was concerned and her stomach churned apprehensively. Gemma had no reason to be jealous; she was going out with Noël. Maybe she was simply speaking the truth.

'There you are.' Brady turned with a smile as she came down the gangplank. 'I was beginning to think you had got lost.'

'Sorry.' She found she couldn't quite look him in the eye. Her heart was racing; her mouth felt dry. She wanted to fling her arms around him and ask him if she could come with him on his business trip. She wanted him to tell her he loved her.

He opened the back door of the limousine and, taking her bag from her, put it inside. Then he caught hold of her arm as she half made to get into the car. 'Hold on, not so fast. I haven't said goodbye.'

She glanced up at him uncertainly and he smiled. 'I'll be back tomorrow night,' he said softly but firmly. 'In the meantime I think you should finish with your boyfriend.'

She frowned, unsure as to how she should take that demand. Was it his way of telling her that he was serious about her? Or was he just laying down the law at the start of a casual affair? 'Are you going to finish with your other women?' she asked tentatively.

He smiled at her. 'What other women?' He swiftly bent and kissed her lips.

The touch of his mouth on hers made her quiver all over. Her hand moved up to the soft material of his jacket as she stood on tiptoe to deepen the kiss.

She was breathless when he stepped back from her. 'Until tomorrow,' he said gently and she nodded and somehow got into the car.

He closed the car door firmly and then it pulled out and drove slowly away along the quayside. Isabella turned and waved to him. He lifted his hand once in a brief kind of salute and then turned to go back on board the boat.

She turned with a sigh and leaned her head back against

the luxurious softness of the car seats. What had she started? The questions raced around and around, sometimes sharp and reproachful, then softly conciliatory. She loved him…had always loved him, but the fact remained that she had had done the one thing that she had sworn would never happen again. She had allowed him into her heart, had left herself open and vulnerable to a man who at the end of the day she didn't really know if she could trust.

The chauffeur stopped outside Brady's house and jumped out to open the car door and also the door of the house for her.

'*Merci.*' Isabella smiled at him and went inside. She felt suddenly tired and a little tearful, in need of a friendly face. She put her bag down on a chair in the hall and made her way through to the kitchen.

The delicious smell of freshly baked bread greeted her. Madame Dupont was just taking it out of the oven. She was listening to a chat show on the radio and talking back to it in a sharply disapproving tone. 'Rubbish,' she was saying crisply in French, 'utter nonsense.'

Isabella smiled. 'Am I intruding?' she asked gently.

'Belle!' The older woman turned and her face lit up with pleasure. 'No of course not, come in, come in.' She cleared a space of her baking equipment at the table and waved her towards a chair. 'I'll make us some coffee.'

'It's all right, I'll make it; you're busy.' Isabella moved over towards the kettle and filled it.

Madame Dupont switched off the radio.

'You don't need to do that,' Isabella told her hastily. 'I don't want to interrupt your programme.'

'Oh, it was rubbish anyway.' The Frenchwoman shrugged her shoulders. 'I would much rather hear how your weekend went.'

'It was all right,' Isabella answered non-committally.

'Just all right?' The woman smiled knowingly. 'Gemma was rather put out that she hadn't been asked to stay overnight as well.'

Isabella frowned. 'Gemma didn't want to stay. She had other plans with Noël.'

'Is that what Brady told you?' Madame Dupont laughed. 'Ah, these men, so transparent!'

It wasn't transparent to Isabella. 'You mean Brady sent her away deliberately so that we would be alone?'

The woman shrugged. 'I only read between the lines,' she said with a glint in her eyes.

The kettle boiled and Isabella turned to make the coffee. She didn't know if she was pleased to hear that Brady had been so calculating about getting her on her own. It was almost as if he had planned her seduction.

'So did you have a good time?' the housekeeper asked again now.

'Yes.' Isabella put the coffee on the table and sat down. 'What do you think of Gemma, *madame*?' she asked impulsively.

The woman smiled disapprovingly. 'She is trouble, a scheming, nasty woman, and I have said as much to Brady on many an occasion.'

Isabella was surprised at such an outburst. 'What does Brady say to that?'

Madame Dupont sipped her coffee and took her time about answering. 'He says nothing. She is an efficient secretary.'

The ring of the telephone interrupted them and the woman got up to answer it. 'It's for you, Belle.' She held over the receiver. 'Your mother.'

Elizabeth Brook sounded agitated. 'It's about your father—'

'He's all right, isn't he?' Immediately cold hands of fear gripped Isabella.

'Yes, yes. Back to his old self. That's what I'm ringing about. He's fussing about the business. You know how he goes on about it. He wants to know how you're progressing with the security side of things.'

'I'm not progressing at all.' Isabella pulled up a stool and sat down.

'Oh, dear. I had hoped to be able to tell him everything was in order. He's been talking about ringing Brady.'

'Brady is in Switzerland until tomorrow night.' Isabella ran an agitated hand through the length of her long hair. 'Look, Mum, try and calm him down about it. Brady and I should be back in London in a few days and we'll talk to him then.'

Isabella replaced the receiver with a heavy heart. She should have spoken to Brady about this before he left. She should have spoken about it right at the start, a little voice whispered inside her. Thinking that Brady was involved in any way with tampering with those perfume reports had been pure folly on her part. She realised now that she had let emotional feelings cloud her real judgement. She had been so afraid of seeing him again and of working with him that she had seized gratefully on the opportunity to be able to keep her emotional barriers up against him.

'Problems?' Madame Dupont interrupted her thoughts and she realised that she had been sitting staring into space for the last few minutes.

'Nothing I can't handle.' Isabella injected a note of confidence into her voice and jumped down from the stool. She would sort it all out with Brady when he returned.

The day seemed to drag by after that. She tried to phone Julien a couple of times, but there was no reply. She didn't know whether to be relieved or worried about that. Gemma had said he had an urgent message for her, which was a little bit perturbing. On the other hand, she had a good idea that it would be no more urgent than just wanting to know when he could see her again. She sighed and went through to the lounge to flick the television on and try and take her mind off things. She was going to have to tell Julien again that it was over between them, and she hated that. He was such a nice guy and he had been so good to her in the past.

She found herself remembering Paris. She had felt so alone when she first arrived there. Her heart had been still hurting over Brady, her father had been angry that she had taken a job in another company instead of his, and in general the whole world had seemed against her.

Then she had met Julien. Her lips curved in a soft smile. He had been wonderful to her, a real friend when she had most needed one.

The doorbell rang, interrupting her thoughts. She frowned and glanced out of the window. It was dark now and she was alone in the house, as Madame Dupont had gone home hours ago. It was so isolated and lonely up here that she was nervous about answering the door when she was alone.

The doorbell rang again, loudly and insistently this time. Whoever was outside was anxious to be let in. Isabella got up and went out into the hall to peer through the small glass panel in the front door.

It was raining heavily outside. A storm had blown up late in the afternoon and it seemed to have settled in for the evening. Every now and then there was a flash of lightning and a low grumble of thunder which added a little to Isabella's nervous mood.

A man stood on the doorstep, dressed in a heavy raincoat, a hat pulled well down over his face. He reached to press the bell again and there was another flash of lightning illuminating his face for just a moment.

Isabella could hardly believe her eyes; for a moment she

thought that she was dreaming. She swung open the door and glanced up at the man.

'Julien! I don't believe it. What are you doing here?'

'Is that any way to greet an old friend?' He stepped inside, a grin on his handsome face as he took off the hat.

The light shone down on his gleaming blond hair, the smooth tanned skin. Even after weathering a raging storm he was as suavely attractive as ever. He took off his coat and tossed it casually over the stand beside him. 'How are you, *chérie*?' He embraced her warmly and kissed her on both cheeks.

'Fine.' She extricated herself from him. 'I just can't believe you are here.'

He frowned. 'Well, I did speak to some woman on the phone yesterday. I got this address from her and said I might call.'

'That was Gemma,' Isabella said with a shake of her head. 'And she never mentioned the fact that you might call.'

'No? I wonder why?' Julien shrugged his shoulders. 'Never mind. I'm here now and you're here. That's all that matters.' Blue eyes moved over her slender body. 'I can't tell you how much I've missed you. Paris isn't the same since you left.'

Isabella laughed nervously. She didn't want Julien to shower her with compliments and tell her how much he missed her. It made it so much harder to make it clear she would not be going back to Paris or to him.

His eyes clouded. 'You are not pleased to see me?' he asked and for a moment his perfect English slipped and he spoke in French. 'Why not, *chérie*? Is there someone else?'

Isabella swallowed hard. 'Of course I'm pleased to see you, Julien,' she answered hesitantly. She linked her arm through his. 'Come on into the lounge and warm up.'

The lounge was warm and cosy-looking. A log fire burned brightly in the grate. 'This is a beautiful house.' Julien glanced around in admiration at the luxurious room.

'Yes, Brady has good taste.' She waved him towards a chair. 'Can I get you a drink?'

'A whisky would be good.' He sat down in the chair next to the fire and watched silently as she crossed to the drinks cabinet.

'You are looking very beautiful,' he said softly as she came back with his drink.

'Thank you.' Feeling awkward, Isabella sat down in the chair opposite. It felt wrong entertaining Julien in Brady's house somehow. But she could hardly send him away without even offering him a drink. He was still her friend, after all. She leaned back in her chair and crossed long legs. 'How come you've managed to get time off work?' she asked, more for something to say than anything else.

'I realised that if I didn't come you would probably go straight back to England and I wouldn't see you at all,' he murmured gently. 'I needed to see you, Isabella; I needed to look you in the eyes and ask you one more time if you would change your mind and be my wife.'

'Oh, Julien.' She shook her head sadly. 'You know I'm fond of you...' She trailed off at a loss. She didn't know what to say to him. He was very dear to her and he always would be, but that was all. She felt no overwhelming passion for him, none of the breathless excitement she felt with Brady.

'So the answer is still the same?' He shook his head. 'When we were apart I hoped that you would realise you missed me, that we were meant for each other.'

'Julien, you know how I feel about you. You are my friend and—'

'And you're very fond of me,' he finished for her bitterly. 'But I want more than that.'

'I know, but I can't offer you more than that.' She shook her head sadly. 'Please understand.'

'Is it Brady?' he asked bleakly.

She hesitated, then nodded; Julien deserved to know the truth. 'Yes. I'm in love with him.'

'I see.' He downed the rest of his whisky and then waved the glass in the air. 'Mind if I have a refill?'

'No.' Isabella got up and poured him another drink. Her hand shook as she held the crystal decanter. She hated so much having to hurt him.

'Where is this Brady?' Julien asked now.

'Away on business.' She returned with his drink and then went to pour herself a glass of wine.

'He's left you alone?' Julien sounded disapproving.

'He will be back tomorrow.' Isabella sat back down and met his eyes steadily. 'I'm sorry if I've upset you, Julien.'

His lips twisted. 'I always knew that you were in love with Brady. I just hoped that the man would not return your feelings.' He shrugged. 'That was a foolish hope, I realise that now.'

'I don't know about that, Julien.' Isabella glanced down at the golden liquid in her glass, her eyes sad. 'I don't know if he does return my feelings.'

'Then the man is an idiot,' Julien said with vehemence.

Isabella laughed, and the tension was released as they both smiled at each other.

'You know I wish you well, *chérie*,' he said gently now.

'Thank you.' Isabella sipped her wine. 'Where are you staying, Julien.'

He shrugged. 'I hadn't got around to that. I just took the first available flight down to Nice and hired a car at the airport. I couldn't think past seeing you.'

'Oh.' Isabella immediately felt guilty. 'I'd like to ask you to stay here, Julien, but it's not my house.'

'That's all right, *chérie*, I'll drive back down to Ste-

Maxime or St Raphaël. I'm sure I'll find somewhere to stay.'

Isabella doubted it very much. It was getting on for eleven o'clock, by the time he got down to Ste-Maxime it would be heading for twelve. It seemed heartless to send him off at midnight when she was alone in a twelve-bedroomed mansion. 'No, Julien, stay here,' she said impulsively. 'There are so many bedrooms here that it seems silly for you to go looking for a hotel.'

'You don't think Brady will mind?' he asked with a rise of his eyebrow.

Isabella grinned. 'Well, he's not here to ask tonight, is he?'

Despite her confident tone Isabella tossed and turned that night, worrying about Julien, about Brady, about everything.

The storm seemed to have become more persistent. Lightning illuminated the darkness of her room and thunder roared insistently. In a way she was glad not to be alone in the house, and Brady hadn't bothered to phone her. Why hadn't he? she wondered again and again. Finally she drifted off into an uneasy sleep.

She awoke to a brilliantly sunny morning. The storm had freshened the air and the heat had returned. Isabella dressed quickly in a forget-me-not-blue summer dress and hurried downstairs.

Julien was out in the pool, swimming backwards and forwards with powerful strokes through the blue of the water.

'Good morning.' Isabella stood next to the edge of the pool and he stopped immediately.

'Good morning, Isabella.' He brushed a hand through his wet hair and grinned at her ruefully. 'You don't mind me taking a swim, I hope?'

'No...no,' she assured him quickly, but there was a part

of her that was uneasy about this. 'Would you like some breakfast?'

'Your housekeeper is making me some.' He continued with his swimming. 'Why don't you come in here and join me?'

'No, Julien. I have to go to the factory today. I have some work to finish. I'll just go and see if Madame Dupont is all right.' Isabella hurried off to the kitchen. She hadn't expected Madame Dupont so early.

She found the woman brewing fresh coffee and arranging cold meats and cheese on a plate. 'Ah, Isabella, this is for your young man,' she said, a frown on her pleasant face as she spoke.

'Well, he is just a friend, *madame*,' Isabella explained hastily. 'I hope it was permissible for me to invite him to stay; he turned up late last night and he had no-where booked...'

'Isabella, you don't need to explain to me.' The woman turned to put everything on a tray. 'I understand perfectly. And anyway, it will be good for Brady.'

'Good for Brady?' Isabella was perplexed.

'Of course. The man is far too complacent. Thinks all women will just wait around for him.' She finished arranging the tray and then turned with a grin. 'Although I must say most of them do. You make a refreshing change.'

Isabella shook her head. '*Madame*, there is nothing between Julien and myself.'

'Of course not. You are in love with Brady, you always have been. But it doesn't do to let Brady know all of your hand.' With a wink the woman carried the tray out of the room.

Isabella followed her with a sinking heart. Were her feelings for Brady really so transparent? The thought made her pride rebel furiously.

Madame Dupont put the tray down on the patio table

and, with another knowing smile at Isabella, disappeared back to the kitchen.

Julien climbed out of the swimming-pool. 'That looks good.' He walked over and picked his towel up to wipe off the excess water from his hair and face.

Isabella sat down and poured them both some coffee. 'What are your plans, Julien? Brady will be home some time today and I don't think it would be a good idea for you to be here.'

'Ah, Isabella, and I was looking forward to seeing this love of your life.' There was no bitterness in his tone as he spoke, just a gleam of good humour.

'Julien, you are incorrigible,' she said with a shake of her head. But inside she was glad that Julien was being so good about things.

'Quite honestly, *chérie*, I would like to see this man. It would put my mind at rest. I'd like to know if he really cares for you, if he will look after you.'

'Julien, I know you mean well, but...'

'But you would rather I didn't stay.' Julien shrugged and sat down to drink his coffee. 'Very well. I'll be going after breakfast.'

There was silence for a moment as they ate Madame Dupont's fresh bread.

'Do you remember that little restaurant we used to go to on the South Bank?' Julien asked suddenly.

She smiled at the memory. 'Of course I do. We had some wonderful evenings in there.'

For a while they reminisced. It was pleasant, sitting out in the sun, laughing and talking about old times. 'They were good days, Julien,' she said as she laughed again with him.

'This sounds like fun; can anyone join in?' The smooth voice from behind startled her. She turned swiftly to see Brady standing in the open French doors.

He was dressed in a dark business suit and there was an expression on his face that was nearly as dark.

'Brady! I wasn't expecting you so soon!' she said, putting down her coffee-cup with a shaky hand.

'Obviously.' He drawled the word, and there was a menacing gleam in his eyes as he came closer across the patio.

CHAPTER EIGHT

JULIEN got sharply to his feet and strode forward towards Brady. 'You must be my absent host,' he said with a smile. 'I'm Julien Arnault.'

'Somehow I thought that was who you were.' Brady took the outstretched hand in a firm handshake. 'I'm pleased to meet you.'

Isabella let out a sigh of relief; for one awful moment she had thought that Brady was going to be annoyed. Instead he was greeting Julien quite pleasantly.

'I thought you wouldn't be home until tonight,' she said to him as he came to sit down at the table with them. She suppressed a feeling of disappointment when he did not come around the table to give her a kiss.

'I decided to take an early flight.' He glanced over at Isabella, but there was no warmth in his dark eyes; they were cool, uncaring almost.

'I hope you don't mind, but Isabella allowed me to stay last night,' Julien cut in. 'I arrived late and I had nowhere to stay so she kindly offered me one of your spare rooms.'

'Why should I mind?' One dark eyebrow lifted as he turned to look at the other man again.

Madame Dupont brought some fresh coffee and an extra cup and saucer at that moment, so Julien was spared having to answer that question.

Brady took off his jacket and leaned back in his chair as he poured himself some coffee.

'How was your business meeting?' Isabella asked him tentatively.

'Enlightening,' Brady muttered abrasively.

Isabella swallowed hard. It was obvious that Brady was not in the best of humours. Was it finding Julien at his home or was there something else?

'Where's Gemma?' she asked, searching desperately to find what was the matter.

'Basle.' Brady glanced at his wristwatch and then sipped his coffee in a hurried manner. 'I have a business call to make. You'll have to excuse me.' Then, without waiting for a reply, he stood up and marched back inside the house.

Julien met her eyes across the table. 'I think that your Brady has other things on his mind apart from you,' he said drily.

Isabella felt like crying, but she managed a determined smile. 'To be honest, Julien, I don't think I'm on his mind at all,' she said softly.

Julien shook his head. 'Ah, well, he is English after all,' he said with a gleam of humour. 'You can't expect him to be as passionate as a Frenchman.'

His remark raised a ghost of a smile.

'Don't worry, Isabella.' Julien stretched out a hand and ruffled her blonde hair with affection. 'No man in his right mind could fail to love you.'

'Thank you, Julien, but you are slightly biased,' she said with a wry smile.

'I am?' He grinned, then stood up. 'I'll have to go and pack up my things. If I set off now I'll be back in Paris in time to go to the hospital for my evening rounds.'

Isabella waited downstairs as Julien went up to shower and change. There was no sign of Brady; he was still in his office, the door firmly closed. When Julien came downstairs again he insisted on going into the office to say goodbye to him. Isabella did not accompany him. She felt

awkward around Brady with Julien here and also she was
unsure of where she stood with him, unsure and very
afraid.

Julien was in Brady's office for only a few minutes. He
reappeared on his own and smiled at Isabella in a wry
fashion when she asked if Brady had said anything.

'By "anything", I take it you mean about you,' he said
sardonically. 'And yes, he did. He asked me if I had a
specific reason for visiting you.'

'Oh?' Isabella came to a halt on the front steps outside
the house. 'And what did you tell him?'

'Well, I told him the truth, of course.' Julien ruffled her
hair and then put an arm around her shoulders. 'Don't look
so worried, *chérie*. Now come along and walk with me to
my car.'

'I wish things could have been different,' Isabella murmured as she walked alongside him.

He squeezed her shoulder. 'Just remember, any time you
need someone I'll be there. All you have to do is pick up
the phone.'

'Thank you, Julien.' She looked up at him and for a
moment her eyes burned with tears. Julien had been such
a dear friend to her and she knew that she would probably
never see him again.

He kissed her briefly on the lips and climbed into his
car. Then the powerful engine roared into action and he
was gone from her life.

'A very touching scene.' The sardonic voice from behind her made her jump. Brady was leaning indolently in
the open doorway of the house. 'When you have collected
yourself, I would like a word with you in my office.' He
turned and strode back into the house, leaving Isabella
standing nervously in the middle of the driveway, her heart
thudding wildly. It was like being summoned to the head-

master's office, only worse, she thought as she went back inside.

His office door was closed and she stood outside it for a few moments, trying to calm her ruffled nerves. Why on earth was Brady acting in such a cold manner towards her? Was he jealous of Julien's presence or was there something else? Was it simply the fact that he was regretting spending the night with her and was now trying to figure a way of getting her to go? Isabella took a deep breath and, holding her head high, went in to face him.

He was sitting at his desk, leafing through a report with impatient fingers. 'Just sit down,' he muttered without looking up immediately.

Isabella sat on the soft leather chair, her blood-pressure starting to rise. How dared he treat her in this cold, uncivilised manner? She had done nothing to deserve this. She glared at the top of his dark hair, memories of the past surfacing, taunting her.

'I have some business matters to discuss with you.' He glanced up abruptly, catching the angry expression on her face.

'Yes?' She remained calm somehow, even managed to sound aloof. It was hard to imagine that only yesterday this man had kissed her with such passion.

The note of indifference in her voice seemed to spark a flame in his dark eyes and for a brief moment he said nothing. Was he jealous? Her hands squeezed into tight fists on her lap. Perhaps he was; perhaps he really cared for her and was just furious at finding Julien here.

Gathering all her courage, she faced him squarely. 'Perhaps business can wait, Brady. Maybe we should talk about us—'

'Us?' He cut across her sharply and there was a sarcastic tone to his voice. 'I think you are mistaken, Isabella. The only thing that we have to discuss is business.'

Isabella flushed from the harsh words, the glimmer of hope inside her starting to die. She shook her head, not wanting to believe what she was hearing. 'Is this…is this anything to do with Julien's visit here? Because—' She started to try and explain that Julien was just a friend, that nothing had happened between them, but he wasn't interested.

'Don't flatter yourself that I give a damn about you and Julien,' he cut across her ruthlessly.

Her face drained of colour and she stared at him wordlessly, her blue eyes filled with an expression of bewilderment. It was as if history was repeating itself. Brady Webster didn't care about her…not in any deep, meaningful way. The dreams that she had tentatively started to nurture started to shatter. There would be no future for her and Brady. Nothing had changed.

'What I really want to know is what the hell you've been playing at within the business,' he rasped furiously.

'Playing at?' She frowned, her mind numbly trying to function as usual, but it was hard, very hard, when her heart felt as if it had just been kicked out of her.

'You know what I'm talking about,' he insisted drily. 'The breach of security at the factory.'

'Oh!' Her eyes widened and she stared at him for a moment in surprise. That was the last thing she had been thinking about at this moment.

'You might well look at me like that,' he growled. 'I had a phone call from your father. He informed me that you've known since you took over about this security matter—that, in fact, I am your number one suspect.'

Isabella swallowed hard. Whatever had possessed Tom to tell him? Imagine informing Brady that she suspected him! 'I'm sorry, Brady.' She spoke with quiet dignity. 'I just didn't know whether I could trust you or not.'

'Hence the furtive glances at important documents.' He glared at her.

'I...I didn't know what to think,' she stumbled, feeling absolutely wretched now. 'You've got to understand that I had to look at the problem rationally. Apart from Claude, who is not suspect, only you, Richard and my father had access to those files. I knew it wasn't Tom and I don't think Richard would have anything to gain by selling the ideas. That left you.'

'And, since I am managing director of a rival company, you automatically thought I would gain more than anyone,' he finished for her acidly. 'But let me tell you that I would have the most to lose.'

'How is that?' She met his eyes directly, trying not to feel guilty about her suspicions, but it was very hard when deep down she knew she had allowed personal feelings to cloud her judgement.

'Would you trust a managing director who stole secrets from his other company?' he enquired in a sarcastically cutting tone. 'Do you really think Wolf-Chem would be happy with the knowledge that their managing director was not entirely honest? Or maybe you think the whole company is corrupt?'

'No of course not,' she replied heatedly.

'Just me?' The dark eyes were bitter with contempt.

It was all a long way from the gentle kiss that he had bestowed on her...was it only yesterday? Isabella's heart thudded painfully. Was it her mistrust that had brought about this change or would it have happened anyway? 'Brady, I'm sorry.' Her blue eyes were wide and unconsciously pleading. 'Maybe I did allow personal feelings to cloud my judgement of you.'

Her apology, far from making matters better, seemed to make them worse for some reason. His features were granite-hard as his eyes moved over her. 'You mean you wanted revenge,' he said drily. 'You must have been disappointed when you couldn't find any incriminating evidence on me. What was your next step, Isabella? Were you going to get close enough to me and then plant some?'

'No!' Her face blanched at such an accusation.

He watched the play of emotions over her face and shrugged. 'I never realised until recently how germane that old saying is... ''Hell hath no fury like a woman scorned''.'

'I wasn't out for revenge, Brady.' Her voice was strained and tense, her eyes implored him to believe her, but the harsh expression on his face never faltered for a moment. It was clear that no matter what she said he would not believe her now.

Silence stretched between them and with it the feeling of hopelessness. 'So what do you suggest we do about the security problem?' She forced herself to sound practical, her hands clenched tightly in her lap.

For a moment he didn't answer. 'I have it in hand,' was all the reply she received.

'Already?' She frowned. 'But surely it will take some time—'

'I have the situation well under control; that is all you need to know, Isabella,' he cut across her drily. 'Now, if you will excuse me, I have work to do.'

Isabella could feel anger bubbling up at this rude, arrogant attitude. She knew she had been wrong not to discuss the security matter with him, but she didn't deserve his coldness. She certainly didn't deserve to be spoken to as if she were still that naïve little eighteen-year-old who was just in the way. 'I have work to do as well, Brady.' Her voice was ice-cold now. 'But I think we should sort this matter out now.'

'Pity that you didn't think like that before,' he grated sardonically. The phone rang beside him and he snatched it up impatiently. 'Yes?' His voice was brisk; a heavy frown marked the handsome features. 'Well, get on with it, then,' he snapped briskly.

Watching him, Isabella felt a chill of fear in her heart. Brady rarely lost his temper, but she could sense that at this moment he was restraining it with difficulty. Whoever was on the other end of that phone was getting the brunt of his displeasure.

He snapped back the receiver and glared across at her. 'We will have to leave for the factory now. Some incompetent fool has mixed up a major order.'

'I see.' Isabella shrugged her slim shoulders. 'Then I suppose we had better go.'

The journey to the factory was a nightmare. Neither of them spoke and the atmosphere was charged with a tense electrical current. Isabella glanced across at him a few times. His face wore a close and angry expression. Whether he was furious about the problem at the factory or just with her she couldn't have said; all she knew was the tremendous relief when he turned through the gates of the factory and pulled to a stop.

She was quick to get out. 'I'll see you later, then,' she said tersely as they walked together towards the main building.

'I suppose so.' He muttered the words drily and strode off in the direction of his office, leaving her fuming with suppressed anger and indignation.

Damn the man. She sat at her office desk and glared at the report in front of her as if it were to blame for Brady Webster's attitude. How dared he be so insensitive, so uncaring? She looked up as the phone on her desk rang and snatched it up briskly.

'Isabella?' Brady's voice had lost none of its ill humour. 'Get yourself into my office for one o'clock.' The words were issued in a clipped, commanding tone that made

Isabella see red. The nerve of the man, speaking to her like that!

'I don't know who you think you are talking to, Brady, but I am not your secretary. Anyway, I am busy,' she answered impulsively. 'I only have a few short reports to deal with and I'm going to try and get a flight home this afternoon.'

Her remark met with total silence for a moment. 'I see,' he drawled coolly. 'To Paris or London?'

She frowned. Why on earth would he think she was going to Paris? 'To London. I have work to attend to.'

'I suppose so,' he agreed drily.

Isabella's heart thudded painfully as he agreed. A small part of her had hoped he would ask her to delay her departure.

'I'll organise the company jet for you,' he said briskly and hung up.

Isabella felt like crying suddenly. If she needed a sure sign that Brady wasn't interested in her that was it. If he had been in any way in love with her he wouldn't have wanted her to go. Instead he was just relieved that she was going to be out of his life for a while. She didn't know who she was the most angry with—herself for being so naïve as to presume he cared anything for her, or him.

She didn't get any work done that morning. In the end, in sheer frustration, she packed the reports away into her briefcase and decided to do the work on them later. Then, gathering up all her courage, she went to face Brady.

She was surprised to find him standing by the window in his office, staring out as if in deep thought. 'Sorry to barge in.' She forced herself to meet his eyes. 'But I've finished and I'd like to go back to the house to pack. Is Bernard anywhere around?' The words came out in a rush. She had the appearance of a young woman in a hurry; there was no hint of the turmoil inside her.

He shrugged and looked at her coldly for a moment. 'I suppose he is.' He crossed to the phone and lifted it to ask his secretary to send the chauffeur up.

'Thanks, I'll wait outside.' Before he could say anything more she left. It was as much as she could do to keep her control for those few moments. She felt wretched; there was a part of her that wanted to fling herself into his arms and plead with him to make everything all right. But her pride would never allow that. She had been humiliated by Brady once…that was quite enough in one young lifetime. Now she would leave on her own terms; at least he had no idea how much she was really hurting inside.

Bernard met her in the corridor and led her out towards the limousine. It was a short journey back to Brady's house, where she threw her few possessions in her bag. It was only then that she realised that she had no idea what time Brady had arranged her flight for, if indeed he had managed to arrange it at all.

She sat down on her bed and glared at the closed suitcase. How foolish of her not to have asked him when she had gone to his office, she chastised herself severely. The fact that she hadn't really been in any fit emotional state to think rationally was no excuse. Brady managed to keep his emotional life and his business life strictly separate; she should be able to do the same. She should have been able to ask him crisply for the details of her flight in the same tone he had used to her earlier. Her lips pursed with determination as she reached for the phone and asked to be put through to him.

It was a shock to be told by his secretary that he had left and wouldn't be back until late afternoon. Typical…Isabella thought as she slammed the receiver down. Brady was so laid-back that he had gone out without even thinking about her. Isabella swallowed down the tearful feeling that threatened to engulf her. There was absolutely no point feeling sorry for herself, she told herself briskly and, lifting up her suitcase, she went downstairs. Maybe Madame Dupont or Bernard would be able to give her the number to check her flight details herself.

She put her suitcase in the hall and went through to the kitchen to find the housekeeper. She came to an abrupt halt when she saw that Brady was with her.

He was sitting at the kitchen table drinking coffee. 'Are you ready?' he asked calmly as if they had arranged to meet here, as if their bitter argument had never taken place.

It took all of Isabella's inner strength to match that nonchalant mood of his, but she was determined to keep up her appearance of being unconcerned. 'Yes, I am. What time do I fly?'

'Four o clock.' Brady glanced at his watch. 'If we leave now we will be in good time.'

'I don't expect you to take me to the airport, Brady.' She was quietly pleased with the matter-of-fact tone to her voice as she calmly walked across to the table to sit down. 'I'm sure Bernard will take me.'

'It's Bernard's afternoon off.' Brady's voice didn't sound quite as relaxed for a moment. 'I told him he could go home. He does have a wife and two children he likes to see on his day off.'

'Oh!' For a moment Isabella was flustered, but quickly regained her composure. 'I will get a taxi,' she snapped.

'I would be pleased to take you,' Madame Dupont offered spontaneously.

'That won't be necessary.' Brady cut across the woman briskly. 'I have some business to see to in Nice anyway, so it is no trouble to drop Isabella at the airport.' With that he stood up.

Isabella also rose to her feet. It seemed that there was no way that she was going to get out of Brady's company for a while. She might as well just go along with him and try to remain as dignified as possible. 'Goodbye, *madame*.' She went across to the woman, who embraced her warmly.

'*Au revoir, chérie*. I'm sure we will be seeing you again very soon.'

Isabella just nodded her head. She felt sure that she would never set foot in Brady's house again. In fact the further away she could get from the man, the better it would be.

'Are you going to Paris, *chérie*?' the housekeeper continued as she walked back with them both towards the front door.

Isabella frowned. Why did everyone seem to assume she was going back to Paris? 'No, London. I must visit my father.'

'Ah, I see.' The woman smiled at her. 'So when will you see Julien again?'

Isabella gave a quick glance at the woman, startled by the question. 'Well, I don't know.' She shrugged. Then, aware that Brady was listening, she tried to salvage some of her pride by saying idly, 'Maybe next month. It won't be long, I'm sure.' She couldn't really say why she told such a blatant lie; she had no intention of seeing Julien next month. It was just some perverse streak of pride that wanted to let Brady know that although he wasn't interested in her emotionally someone else was.

'He seemed a very pleasant young man,' Madame Dupont said with a knowing look at Brady's back as he preceded them out to the car.

'Yes he is.' Isabella wished fervently that the subject would be changed. She felt most uncomfortable about it and there was a strong feeling of guilt that she had just told such a blatant lie.

'I hope I'll get an invitation to the wedding,' Madame Dupont continued in a jovial tone.

The remark met complete silence for a moment. Isabella

knew the woman was only joking, but in the circumstances Isabella felt unable to take the light-hearted teasing in a good humour. 'You'll be first on my invitation list,' she said stiffly, then, reaching the car, she wrenched open the door and climbed in. 'Goodbye, *madame*, and thank you for looking after me so well.'

'It is always a pleasure to see you.'

They left the woman waving madly until Brady's car disappeared out of the gates and down the twisty narrow road.

Inside Isabella felt sick and there was a certain element of fear at being so close to Brady. She just wanted to be away from him now; she didn't know how long she would be able to keep up this cool façade of the tough, uncaring woman, when in fact she felt like an emotional wreck.

The drive to the airport was completed in almost total silence. It was a beautiful afternoon; the unsettled weather of the previous day had completely gone and now the sun shone down fiercely from a cornflower-blue sky.

'Are you going back to the factory this afternoon?' Isabella asked, striving for a normal conversation, as he pulled into the entrance to the airport. She wanted him to think she didn't care that he didn't want her; even though her heart was hurting more than she could bear she held her head up high and turned to look at him.

'I might.' Instead of just dropping her off, he went to find a parking place.

'You really don't need to come in with me,' she said hurriedly, but it was too late; he had found a place and was pulling into it.

'Come on, I'll carry your bag.' He climbed out and she was left with no choice but to walk with him into the terminal.

They checked her bag in and then Brady looked at his watch. 'You have half an hour to wait,' he said crisply.

'That's all right, Brady,' Isabella said hurriedly. 'You go; there's no point waiting around here. I'm sure you have business to attend to.'

'I do, but not for another few minutes.' His eyes moved over the curve of her face, the over-bright defiant sparkle in her beautiful blue eyes. 'Come on, I'll buy you a drink,' he said briskly and strode forward towards the refreshment bar.

Isabella frowned. This was ridiculous. It was obvious the man couldn't wait to be rid of her; why was he hanging around here?

She allowed him to buy her a hot chocolate and they sat opposite each other across one of the small tables. A few moments passed without either of them speaking. Isabella watched him furtively from beneath long lashes. He seemed preoccupied with something. His dark features were closed; a pulse beat every now and then at the side of his strong jawline.

'Brady...' she began and then faltered to a halt as his dark eyes glowered straight at her.

'Yes?' For a moment that ice-cool manner seemed to disappear and he just sounded angry.

'I...I was just going to say that there is no need for you to waste your time here. I'll be all right on my own.'

'I'm sure you will.' He sipped his coffee but made no move. 'Will you be at the Brook Mollinar offices tomorrow?' he asked suddenly.

She shrugged. 'I suppose so. I have a lot of work to get on with.'

'Right, well, there are a few things I want you to look into for me.' He then proceeded to reel off a long list of work for her.

'What is this, Brady?' she burst out in annoyance. 'I think I had to point out to you only this morning that I'm a director in the company, not your secretary. Get Gemma to do those things for you.' The nerve of the man, she thought furiously. First he had used her on a physical level, now this. Did the man have no grain of conscience when it came to taking advantage of her?

One dark eyebrow lifted at her outburst. 'It may have escaped your notice, Isabella, but directors have to work hard as well,' he informed her in a scathing tone.

'I'm well aware that I have a big workload; I just hadn't realised that I had to do your work as well. I'm not here to take orders from you, Brady.' Her hands clenched into tight fists. Right at this moment she felt like hitting the man.

'You are new on the board, Isabella.' There was a firm, steel-like quality in his voice, an underlying hint of a threat. 'As yet you are an unknown quantity to the other members. Let's just say it would be prudent to listen to me.'

Isabella stared at him with wide eyes. 'I suppose that's your way of letting me know that you could make things very difficult for me,' she said bitterly.

He shrugged lazily. 'Let's say it would be in your best interests to keep me on your side.'

Isabella glared at him speechlessly. Of all the arrogant, tormenting men she had ever met he was surely the worst.

'So you know what to do when you get into the office?' He started to remind her, and she glared at him.

'Would you like me to take shorthand notes?' she asked in a mocking tone.

'Only if you have difficulty remembering,' he answered smoothly, ignoring her sarcasm.

'Oh, I'll remember,' she murmured bitterly. 'Don't worry, Brady, I'll remember.'

For a moment a brief look of amusement flashed across his features. 'Good, I can see that we will work together beautifully after all.'

Her eyes glittered furiously at his patronising tone. 'And while we are on the subject of business, perhaps you would like to tell me what you are doing about our security problem?' she ground out bitterly.

'We haven't got a security problem,' he answered calmly, then glanced at his watch. 'Right, I'll get going.'

'Now that is a good idea,' Isabella muttered sarcastically. 'But before you do, would you mind telling me what you mean by that ridiculous comment? Of course we've got a security problem; someone went through Claude's files.'

'And I know exactly who that person is,' Brady murmured calmly as he rose to his feet. 'So there is no problem.'

Isabella was struck speechless. How could Brady possibly know who it was? He had only learnt about the whole thing yesterday!

'Have a good journey home and I'll see you in a couple of days' time.' He turned to leave and Isabella found her voice sharply.

'Hold on one minute. How do you know who has been going through those files?' she demanded to know.

He turned with a sardonic look in his dark eyes. 'If you had come to me in the first place, Isabella, you would have discovered that I have known all along about the security breach.'

She stared at him, completely astonished. 'You never said anything about it!'

'I had my reasons,' he said drily.

They were calling Isabella's name over the Tannoy system now, but she made no move. Heat was slowly building up inside her in a furious wave. Why hadn't he told her anything about this?

'They're calling your flight,' Brady said calmly.

'To hell with my flight. Why didn't you tell me you

knew about this? And how dare you haul me over the coals for not mentioning it, when you did the very same thing?'

'Not quite.' His voice was dry. 'I didn't suspect you. There is a difference.'

'So why didn't you discuss the problem with me?' She refused to let the subject drop.

'If you really want to know, I was going to that night at the boat,' he grated harshly. 'But somehow I got sidetracked.'

Her face flared with colour at those sardonic words.

They were calling her name again, more insistently this time. Somehow Isabella got to her feet and picked up her bag.

'Belle.' He caught hold of her arm as she made to move past him. 'Hold on a minute.'

She looked up at him with eyes that shimmered with rage. 'I wouldn't hold on for even a second for you,' she told him bitterly. Then, with her head held high, she walked away.

CHAPTER NINE

ISABELLA stared out at the miserable English weather. It was raining again. Since she had come back from France it didn't seem to do anything else. Still, it suited her mood, grey and miserable.

She had been home for three days now, plenty of time for her to reflect on everything, and one thing was clear: Brady felt nothing for her. Their night together had been just a fling for him. The reality hurt her incredibly. Brady, Brady, Brady... Her mind was filled with him; her body ached for him. She felt totally mixed up.

Why was she so vulnerable and foolish where that man was concerned? she asked herself miserably. She was alternatively angry with herself and then near to tears as the reason came so very clearly to her that she still loved him.

There was a knock at the door and she looked back from the dreary view to the luxurious interior of her office. 'Come in.'

'Sorry to interrupt.' Richard marched in, looking very red in the face and anything but sorry.

'That's all right.' Isabella leaned her head back against the soft leather of her chair. 'Have you a problem?'

'Yes, nothing personal, but I can't agree this different packaging you've suggested for the new perfume.'

'Can't you?' Isabella managed a light, jovial tone when in fact she was at screaming point. Richard had been in and out of her office all morning. If she hadn't known better she would have thought he was being deliberately difficult. 'I have already shown them to our chief marketing manager. He saw no problem.'

'Ah, well, in all honesty Ted Roberts has not been with us long enough to realise his mistake.'

'Ted is very good at his job,' Isabella said in a patient tone. 'He has had many years' experience dealing with big companies.'

'But, like you, he is relatively new to us,' Richard continued stubbornly. 'Anyway, I shall bring the subject up at the board meeting this afternoon. I'm sure the other members of the board will agree with me.'

Isabella shrugged. 'By all means bring it up.'

'Yes, I will. I've already mentioned it to Brady,' Richard continued heatedly.

'You've spoken to Brady?' The man had her full attention now. 'When?' she asked sharply.

'This morning. He rang confirming that he would be attending the meeting this afternoon.'

Brady had rung this morning and hadn't bothered to speak to her. It was crazy to be upset, but she couldn't help it. Of course he hadn't asked to speak to her...why should he? she rationalised sternly. She was probably the last person he would want to talk to.

'Do you know if there is anything important on the agenda for this meeting, Isabella?' Richard interrupted her thoughts, his voice brisk, yet there was a tinge of worry in it.

'Not that I know of,' she said with a shrug.

Richard gave her a strange look. 'I thought as you had seen Brady only a few days ago he might have mentioned something about this afternoon.'

'No, he said nothing.' Isabella glanced down at the work in front of her on the desk. 'I didn't even know he was going to attend the meeting until you told me.' Her voice was flat and she tried very hard not to show how much she cared about that fact.

'Well, I thought you of all people would have been better informed,' Richard muttered irritably. With that he turned and left.

Isabella looked up at the closed door, a thoughtful expression on her face. Purposefully she tried to push her hurt over Brady to the back of her mind and concentrate on facts. She presumed that Brady would have something to say about the security surrounding the new perfume today. Was that why Richard was so tense and angry? Did he have something to do with that break-in? He was the only person left to suspect and he had had the opportunity, but what about the motive? She had racked her brain, but she still couldn't come up with a reason for Richard to do such a terrible thing.

With a sigh she turned her attention back to her work. It wasn't a very productive morning; what with Richard's interruptions and the thought of seeing Brady again, her concentration had deserted her. She finished early for her lunch break. She wasn't hungry, so instead of going for a meal she went to the hairdresser's. Nothing to do with wanting to look her best for Brady, she told herself forcibly as she studied her reflection in the mirror; she just needed the relaxation.

She emerged an hour later feeling much better. Her blonde hair gleamed with good health, its shape altered slightly to frame her face.

She collided with Brady in the lobby of the Brook Mollinar offices. Her head was down and she didn't see him coming out of the lift until she practically walked into him. He reached out a hand to steady her, and she stepped back as if electrified as she glanced up at the dark, handsome features.

'Good afternoon, Belle.' His voice was dry and there

was a sardonic twist to his lips as he noticed how quickly she had moved away from the sudden contact with him.

'Good afternoon, Brady,' she replied stiffly, trying to pretend that he was just some stranger who meant nothing to her.

His eyes moved over the gleaming style of her hair, the soft curve of her lips, and there was a moment's pause.

Isabella's heart seemed to turn over in that instant. It pounded wildly against her chest; her mouth felt dry. There was a look in those dark eyes that almost seemed to suggest that he was glad to see her.

'I've read your report on the packaging for the new perfume.' His voice was cold and crisp and it sent reality racing in a cold shower through her veins.

Of course Brady wasn't glad to see her; he was thinking about business. Disappointment was so overwhelming that for a moment she couldn't find her voice. 'Have you?' She somehow managed to sound vaguely uninterested. 'Well, I haven't time to discuss it now. I have a lot of work to see to before the meeting this afternoon.' She stepped around him hurriedly before her composure cracked, and made towards the lifts. Luckily there was one waiting for her, so she was able to step inside and close the door quickly.

She leaned her head back against the wall as it ascended to the top floor. Seeing him again was pure torture. She couldn't cope with the wealth of emotions he seemed to stir up inside her. Anger and then love wrestled intensely for first position, making her feel almost dizzy. She had to allow her anger against him to win, she kept telling herself resolutely; it was the only way she was going to be able to deal with him. If she thought about how much she loved him, everything would be lost, including the little dignity she had left.

The lift doors opened on the top floor and she walked

down to her office with a brisk, steady pace. She wouldn't think any more about Brady, she told herself firmly. Not one more thought about him would cloud her mind.

She had just seated herself behind her desk in her office when he strode in behind her without knocking.

She glared up at him fiercely. This was intolerable; how could she possibly function with any kind of efficiency when he was barging in on her? 'What do you want now?' Her voice dripped with the kind of barely disguised anger that would have made a lesser man turn tail.

Brady met the full glare of her beautiful eyes head-on. He looked calm and in full control; strangely his air of authority was more chilling than any furious reply he might have made.

He put his briefcase on the floor and leaned his hands on the desk, taking his time to answer her. 'Don't take that tone with me, Isabella,' he warned in an ominously low voice, 'because I can assure you that if you want to be unpleasant you will come off worst.'

Isabella didn't doubt that for one second. Brady wasn't the type of man you deliberately took on expecting to win. She sat back in her chair and took a deep breath. 'I'm trying to work.' Her voice was a lot more controlled now.

'I'm glad to hear it.' His voice was ice-cold. 'Did you get through the list of things I asked you to see to?'

'Yes, I did,' Isabella answered through clenched teeth. The man had a damn nerve, speaking to her like some errant employee. She looked away from him and down towards the report she had been working on before lunch, hoping that, like Richard this morning, he would take the hint and leave. She flicked over it, scanning the pages in a businesslike way, without really seeing them at all. 'Now if there is nothing else…?' she murmured without glancing back up at him.

'Yes, there is.' His voice had a clipped edge that told

her very plainly that she was pushing her luck. He picked up his briefcase from the floor and opened it briskly. 'I'd like you to type up these reports for me.' He dropped a stack of papers on to her desk, causing her to look up at him very quickly.

'You must be joking!' She was outraged at such audacity. 'I have enough work to plough through as it is. Get Gemma to type them up.'

'I can't,' he replied calmly. 'I sacked Gemma last Monday.'

Isabella stared at him incredulously for a moment, all personal feelings forgotten. 'You sacked Gemma? Why on earth did you do that?'

'Because she was the person who went through Claude's reports on the new perfume,' he replied bluntly.

To say that Isabella was thunderstruck was putting it mildly. She just stared at him for a while, too surprised to say anything.

'So,' he continued on calmly, 'in the absence of my secretary I want you to see to these.'

Isabella shook her head; she couldn't think of anything at the moment except this new revelation. 'Why would Gemma steal Claude's ideas?' she asked in a stunned tone.

One dark eyebrow lifted. 'Why does anyone steal anything?' he drawled sardonically. 'For money.' He tapped the stack of files that he had just placed on her desk in a brisk manner. 'Now I want you to get straight on with this.'

Isabella bristled furiously at his manner. 'Get one of the girls up from the typing pool to sort it out,' she told him in no uncertain terms.

Brady shook his head and his dark eyes glittered with a bitter kind of anger. 'These are top-secret files,' he muttered in a dry tone. 'And, as you know, it's hard to discern who to trust these days with such work.'

She felt herself colouring up at those words. She knew it was a dig at the way she had suspected him in the past, and in all honesty she knew deep down that he had every right still to be annoyed with her over that.

'Anyway,' he continued briskly, 'most of the files are in French, and as you are completely fluent in the language you can deal with it until I get somebody better.'

'I see.' For a moment anger rippled through Isabella. She didn't care for his attitude at all. The words 'until I get somebody better' grated unbearably on her tender nerves. 'I suppose I should thank you for the vote of confidence,' she said in a dry tone.

One dark eyebrow lifted. 'Well, it is more than you afforded me,' he answered curtly. Then he turned and left her, the door closing with a quiet finality behind him.

Her eyes flicked from the door to the stack of work he had left for her. Obviously he was still angry with her for not trusting him over the perfume fiasco, but did that really give him the right to treat her like some second-class citizen? How dared he snap orders at her and look at her with such cool, disparaging eyes? Was his attitude generated by her distrust or was it more a case that he just had no respect for her? That idea made her eyes shimmer with tears.

Damn the man. She glared back at the work in front of her, and it was now just a hazy blur of jumbled words dancing before her eyes. How could she have allowed herself to fall in love with him so totally?

She picked up the stack of work that he had left and dropped it into the drawer of her desk, slamming it shut and locking it with a fiercely angry movement. 'I don't love you.' She said the words aloud in a kind of hopeless attempt to lie to herself about her feelings, and promptly just felt foolish... She had been lying to herself for years where Brady was concerned, and look where it had got her.

She tried very hard after that just to dedicate all her thoughts to her work, firmly closing out Brady. It was only when it was nearly time for the afternoon's board meeting that her brain once more was overtaken with a kind of nervous panic.

This was no good, she told herself firmly as she opened her handbag and re-applied some rose-pink lipstick to her lips. She was going to have to get used to Brady's presence; she couldn't spend her days jumping nervously every time she had to come into contact with him. With her head held high she marched down towards the boardroom.

He was already there, taking control in that capable manner of his that made Isabella feel even more on edge. She sat down at the long, polished table and looked around at the other men. Some of them nodded at her, but no one smiled.

Did any one of these men like her ideas or, like Richard, were they all against her? Nerves spiralled inside her and she drummed her fingers against the printed agenda in front of her. She had a horrible suspicion that her efforts would be very much under scrutiny today.

Brady called order and sat at the top of the table. Immediately there was complete silence. She glanced up at him and for a moment their eyes clashed, just as they had done at that first board meeting. On this occasion, however, there was a subtle difference. This time Isabella had no doubts about Brady's capabilities and suddenly she knew that if he wanted to crush her he could very easily turn all these men against her. Her spine stiffened; she would show them she was no push-over.

They dealt with the small items on the agenda first. Then they reached Isabella's ideas about the new packaging for the perfume.

'You have all seen the proposals.' Brady glanced down the long table. 'Would anyone like to comment?'

Isabella's heart pounded as his dark eyes travelled over each of the men, and there was a deathly silence.

'Yes, I have something to say.' Richard spoke as Brady's eyes descended down on him. 'I really don't care for Isabella's ideas at all.'

Brady nodded. 'Would you like to tell us why not?'

'Certainly.' Richard glanced down at some notes that he had made before launching into the attack.

He seemed to go on forever; nothing was right with the packaging as far as he was concerned. 'Forgive me, Isabella, but I'm not surprised that your concepts are wrong,' he finished heatedly. 'You are too young to be able to deal with this.'

Isabella retained her cool with difficulty. 'As I told you earlier,' she replied crisply, 'our top marketing manager has looked at the ideas and approved them.'

'Well, our marketing manager has not been with us long enough to know better,' Richard exploded. He then turned to Brady appealingly. 'I think you must agree with me, Brady,' he muttered, an angry light in his eyes.

Isabella waited with a feeling of anger for Brady to take the opportunity to go against her.

He pursed his lips and there was a moment of silence as everyone waited for him to speak. 'I have spent the last couple of hours going over these ideas with Ted Roberts,' he said in a dry tone, 'and I can only say that I can find no fault with them. Ted may be new to us, as is Isabella, but they are spot-on with their work.'

There was a murmur of approval from the other men at the table. Isabella glanced around in surprise. Obviously Brady's comments met with agreement. She was surprised at such support from the other men, but astounded that Brady should be so steadfastly on her side.

'So you are not going to take my advice on this?'

Richard looked furiously around at the other members of the board.

'What is your problem, Richard?' Brady grated harshly. 'Isabella is doing a first-class job; we are damned lucky to have her.'

'Damn it all, Brady, I have put thirty years of my life into this business. I should know what I'm talking about,' Richard snapped angrily. His eyes were bitter as he glanced down the table. 'I have helped to make this company what it is today; surely that is worth some consideration?'

'Of course it is,' Brady agreed smoothly. 'I have listened to each point you have made, Richard, but the fact remains that the company desperately needs fresh, innovative ideas and Isabella has them.' Brady flicked over the pages in front of him, a serious look on his dark, handsome features. 'I think if we make the changes she is suggesting our perfume will appeal to the younger end of the market as well as the older. We will in fact double our sales.'

Brady sat back in his chair, transferring his attention to the other members of the board. 'Has anyone else anything to say on the matter?'

There was an unanimous murmur of approval for the new ideas almost immediately. Brady returned hard, uncompromising eyes to Richard, 'If you are not happy you can always resign...which quite frankly would be very sad. You are a valuable member of our team, Richard... We would hate to see you go.'

Richard sat up very straight in his chair. 'I'm not thinking of going anywhere,' he said in a voice that wasn't quite steady.

'Good, then maybe we can carry on.' Brady turned the pages on his file briskly. 'About the new perfume...'

The meeting dragged on for another half an hour as new ideas were discussed. Isabella found it hard to give her

attention to it all. She was shaking inside after all the unpleasant accusations from Richard. It was a relief when
Brady glanced at his watch and suggested that they call it
a day.

Richard was the first to leave the room; he looked ready
to strangle someone as he briskly packed his things away,
ignoring everyone. It was a relief when he marched out.
Isabella's hands shook slightly as she packed her papers
into her briefcase. She hated scenes and at the back of her
mind there was the insecure feeling that maybe Richard
had a point.

'You all right, Belle?' Brady's voice interrupted her
thoughts. She glanced up and nodded briefly, but there was
a light in her blue eyes that told him she was anything but
all right.

He waited for her as she finished packing her things
away, then grabbed hold of her arm as she made to leave
the room.

'Belle?' He spoke in a low tone. 'Perhaps you would
like me to drop you home?'

About to refuse, Isabella suddenly changed her mind.
She had been taking the train into work this last week in
order to have time to study the day's work before she
reached the office. Right now she was in no mood to face
the crowded platforms and she certainly wasn't in the
mood to concentrate on any more work.

'Thank you, Brady.' She glanced up at him, surprised
by his gentle manner, and faintly suspicious.

'Good, come on, then.' He retained his hold of her arm.
'I have my chauffeur waiting outside.'

For once the feeling of his hand on her arm didn't cause
her to pull away. It was a relief to have him to lean on.

They walked down to Reception and got into the
stretched limousine in silence.

Isabella looked out at the crowded London streets. It

was rush-hour; everyone was dashing madly to be out of the city. Where were they all going? she wondered, and for a moment she felt herself slipping into a feeling of loneliness. It was as if everyone had a purpose, had a person to rush home to, except her.

'I wouldn't let it worry you.' Brady spoke briskly and she looked around at him with enquiring eyes. 'I had the same problem with Richard when I joined the company. He resents change.'

'Does he?' Isabella glanced down at her hands. 'You don't think he might have a point?'

'Don't be ridiculous!' Brady sounded outraged. 'I might be a lot of things, Isabella, but one thing I am is honest.' He slanted a wry look at her. 'Or maybe you still have difficulty believing that?'

She shook her head quickly. She wanted to tell him once again how sorry she was for ever doubting his business integrity, but he was continuing briskly.

'If I thought you couldn't cope with the job I would want you out.'

Of course he would, she realised suddenly. 'Sorry, Brady, it has been a long day. I think I just let Richard get to me in there.'

Brady shrugged broad shoulders. 'It happens to the best of us. Business can be very cut-throat, especially when it gets to boardroom level.' There was a heavy note of fatigue in the deep voice for a moment, which caused Isabella to glance over at him curiously.

'I haven't had a perfect week myself.' He gave her a brief, lop-sided smile. 'But, personal feelings aside, I think you make one hell of a company director.'

'Thanks, Brady.' She glanced away from him and had to blink back the tears. In other words, he might not have such a high view of her personally, but in business he couldn't fault her. She had got the message.

The car drew up outside her parents' home and she quickly tried to pull herself together. 'Thanks for the lift, Brady.'

'You're welcome.' His voice returned to the cool, clipped tones he had used on her earlier. 'I don't suppose I will see you again for a while. I fly back to France tomorrow morning.'

'Oh?' Her voice was flat as a strange kind of disappointment swept through her. She couldn't bear the thought of him going away, yet it was sweet torture having him around. She felt so mixed up inside. One part of her wanted to throw her arms around him and beg him not to go, the other was telling her in cold terms that Brady didn't care about her at all and she would only make a complete fool of herself.

'Anyway…' His eyes moved over the pale softness of her skin, the wide blue eyes. 'Despite everything, I only wish you the best, Belle.'

'Thank you.' She swallowed hard and reached for the car door-handle; she had to get away from him before she broke down.

She turned to close the door behind her. Brady gave her a brief kind of salute, then he leaned forward and tapped the glass partition in front of him. The powerful car moved away with a smooth acceleration down the drive and out on to the road.

'Is that you, honey?' her father's voice called to her as she stepped through the front door.

'Yes.' She rubbed a shaking hand over the shimmer of tears that threatened to fall. She was so angry with herself for feeling like this; it was crazy to love someone who felt nothing for you. Crazy and self-destructive. She desperately tried to pull herself together, and moved through to the lounge, where Tom and Elizabeth were reading the day's newspapers.

'How did your day go, sweetheart?' Tom looked over at her with a smile.

'It was OK.' Isabella shrugged. She didn't feel up to going into details.

'Only OK?' Tom's eyes were sharp on her pale features. 'Brady told me that you had a major board meeting this afternoon. I hope Richard wasn't too painful. He can be a drag when it comes to making any new changes.'

'He was a bit difficult.' Isabella dismissed the subject, more interested in Brady's visit than anything else. 'You've seen Brady?' she asked sharply.

Tom nodded. 'He called this morning.'

'He never mentioned it to me.' Isabella felt that prickle of hot tears behind her eyelids as she went on. 'He goes back to France tomorrow.'

'Yes, he told me.' Tom's voice was suddenly gentle. 'He also told me how upset he was about that security problem at the factory.'

Isabella nodded. 'He was furious with me for suspecting him; he still is.'

'I think he was a little hurt,' Tom said softly. 'He seems to have the idea that you dislike him intensely. I tried to tell him differently, but he wouldn't have it.'

'I think you have it the wrong way around, Tom,' Isabella murmured in a low voice. 'It's Brady who dislikes me. Or maybe ''despises'' would be a better word to describe his feelings towards me.'

Tom shook his head. 'I think you have that wrong. He spoke about you in glowing terms this morning.' He looked over towards his wife. 'Didn't he, Elizabeth?'

'Oh, yes.' Elizabeth nodded her head. 'In fact he left you a present. I put it up in your room.'

'Did he?' Isabella was quite frankly astonished by this. She didn't wait to continue the conversation, but headed straight for her room, her mind filled with curiosity.

The package that lay on her bed was rather large. Isabella sat down next to it and opened it with trembling fingers. Her heart was beating loudly as she finally peeled back the tissue wrappings and surveyed the beautiful picture of St-Tropez harbour that she had admired so much. There was a brief note with it in Brady's flowing handwriting.

Hope this painting brings back as many happy memories for you as it does for me. I wish you only the very best in life, love, Brady.

Isabella read the message and looked at the painting and promptly gave in to the tears she had been trying so hard not to shed. The words had such a final ring about them.

She didn't know how long she sat just staring at that colourful picture through a hazy blur. The room gradually plunged into darkness as the daylight came to an end, yet still she sat there. In her mind's eye she could see that beautiful harbour so clearly again, smell the salty tang of the fresh air, feel Brady's arms closing about her body, feel his lips pressing against her in a fierce yet wonderfully possessive way. If only he loved her... Her heart yearned to believe that what they had shared had been nothing less than true love, that perhaps the painting meant something to him as well. Then on impulse she reached for her car keys. She had to see Brady one more time before he left; she had to tell him how she felt.

CHAPTER TEN

ISABELLA had never visited Brady's London house before, but she knew exactly where it was. Her father had pointed it out to her once, a long time ago, and she had not forgotten.

It was just outside the city, a tall, impressive-looking house, its garden backing out on to the River Thames. Isabella remembered thinking how lovely it looked, how much character it possessed. Tonight, however, as she turned her car through the darkened gateposts, her heart was beating with tension, her thoughts far from the beauty of the house.

It had taken a good hour to reach her destination, time when she had been racked with indecision. When she finally stepped out of her car into the indigo blackness of the night she noticed two other cars parked to one side of the drive. One she recognised as Brady's; the other was unfamiliar to her. Did Brady have a guest…a woman, perhaps? She paused by the front doorstep, suddenly feeling incredibly foolish.

What on earth was she doing here? How on earth could she have contemplated throwing herself at Brady? No doubt he would find the fact that she had read so much into a mere painting of St-Tropez highly amusing. If he wasn't otherwise occupied he might even take her to bed, but tomorrow in the cool light of day he would order her out. He had shown her quite clearly that he was not interested in a serious relationship with her. Her pride rebelled against the weak feelings of love she felt for him and she half turned away to get back in her car.

The door opened at that moment and a warm flood of golden light spilled over her.

'Belle!' Brady's deep voice sounded as stunned as she felt. 'What are you doing here?'

She looked up into his dark eyes. What could she say...I was just passing? Ludicrous when he knew he lived miles out of her way.

'Is everything all right?' He came forward and caught hold of her arm to lead her inside. She was conscious as she stood under the bright light of his hallway that her eyes were streaked with tears; she probably looked an utter sight.

'Yes, Brady.' She tried very hard, but her voice sounded as unsteady as she felt.

'Come on in.' He opened the door through to a lounge. There was no one else in the magnificent room. A fire blazed in a large Adam fireplace and music was playing in a low, soothing tone from a CD player. He waved her towards the white settee with its rows of gold scatter cushions and went over to the drinks cabinet to pour her a brandy.

He had been working, she noticed absently; a stack of files sat on a low coffee-table.

'Don't you ever take any time off?' she enquired, more for something to say than anything else.

'Only when I have something better to do, and I didn't until now.' He gave her that lop-sided grin that was so attractive and came across to hand her her drink. 'So, what brings you here at this hour?' he asked briskly.

She took a sip of her drink and nearly choked on the fiery liquid as nerves seemed to make her throat close up. 'I...I just wanted to see you before you left tomorrow.'

'I'm glad,' he said quietly, causing her eyes to fly towards his immediately.

There was silence for a moment as their eyes held.

'I don't think I thanked you properly for standing up for me today,' she murmured at last, not wanting to mention the painting immediately, for some reason. Strange how she could have all those brave ideas about flinging herself into his arms and then when she actually came to look him in the eye her heart somersaulted into her boots in terror.

'You drove all the way out here to say that?' One dark eyebrow lifted.

'Well, no…' She took another sip of her drink, feeling most uncomfortable. 'I want to thank you for your gift and…I suppose I just wanted to clear the air between us. I'm sorry, Brady. I'm sorry about suspecting you over the perfume.' She took a deep gulp of air and rushed on. 'And I've missed you terribly since I've come back to London.'

For a moment she didn't think he was going to answer her; he just stared at her.

'What about Julien?' he asked, and there was a heavy tone to his voice now.

'What about him?' She didn't know what reaction she had expected from her statement, but it certainly wasn't cool questions about Julien.

'He told me that he had asked you to marry him, that you were thinking about it, and he was quietly confident.' He picked up his drink from beside his papers and dashed back the remainder of the golden liquid.

'What?' She glared at him as if he had suddenly gone mad.

'He told me quite clearly that day in my study before he left,' Brady went on in a brisk tone.

'I don't care what he told you,' she answered him heatedly and without really thinking. 'Yes, Julien has asked me to marry him, but I never had to think about it…the answer was no. I'm not in love with Julien; I'm in love with...' She trailed off, stopping herself before she could actually commit her emotions to words. 'Well, anyway...' She shrugged, feeling embarrassed now. 'I'm not in love with Julien.'

For a moment there was no expression whatsoever on Brady's dark face, then his lips twisted into a semblance of a smile as he raked a hand through his hair. 'God, Belle, I can't believe you've just said that. I—'

Before he could carry on the door opened into the lounge and a woman walked in. For a moment Isabella thought she was seeing things. It was as if time had raced back and she was just eighteen again and faced with an unexpected and very beautiful rival for Brady's love.

'Bobby!' Her voice dropped like a lead weight into the silence of the room.

'Well, well, I hardly recognised you.' Roberta Webb was the first to regain her composure. Sharp green eyes raked over Isabella's appearance, noting everything from the superb cut of her Chanel suit to the soft, vulnerable light in her eyes. 'Where are your glasses, dear?' she purred. 'As I remember it, you used to be as blind as a bat.'

'I'm wearing contact lenses.' Somehow Isabella faced the woman squarely, although inside she was dying a million deaths. For this woman to appear just after she had so nearly poured her heart out to Brady was the last straw. She felt humiliated and so hurt that it was difficult to breathe. She had known that there was a good chance that Brady would reject her, and even managed to prepare herself for that, but that he was still seeing this woman was heart-breaking.

Roberta was every bit as beautiful as when Isabella had last seen her in the South of France. Her red hair was a little more of a strawberry blonde colour now; it complemented the pale whiteness of her skin and the huge green of her eyes. She was wearing a short green skirt and a black polo-neck sweater that did incredible things for her slender figure. She moved towards the settee and sat down, crossing long legs in a relaxed manner, as if she was settling down for the evening.

Isabella immediately got to her feet. 'Well, I have to be going.' She said the words in a rush and didn't dare even look at Brady.

'You are not going anywhere.' His voice was deep and authoritative as he also rose to his feet. 'Roberta, on the other hand, was just leaving.'

'But...but darling, I haven't finished saying what I came to say,' Roberta burst out, her cool manner ruffled now.

Isabella flinched at the familiar way the other woman was talking to Brady; every word seemed to be like a stick going sharply across her heart. 'It's all right, really,' she hastily interrupted, and moved towards the door. 'I have to go now anyway.'

As she reached to take a hold of the door-handle Brady swiftly caught hold of her hand. 'You are not going anywhere.' He squeezed her hand in a firm yet strangely reassuring way. 'I have things I want to say to you.'

Isabella swallowed hard. She wasn't at all sure she wanted to hear what Brady had to say to her; she felt she had made enough of a fool of herself for one evening.

'But Brady...' there was a note of panic in Roberta's voice for a moment. 'I do so want to explain,' she carried on in a cooler tone.

'There is nothing you can say to me, Bobby.' He turned to face the other woman now and there was a gleam of anger just below the surface. 'You will have to save your explanations for the board of directors' meeting next week.'

The woman seemed to blanch an even whiter shade.

'Surely you don't mean it, darling?' Her bottom lip trembled.

'I mean every word,' Brady grated harshly. 'And don't bother to turn on the tears again, because it just won't work.'

Immediately the other woman's face hardened. 'Well, if that is the way you want to play it.' She stood up and her whole body seemed to tremble with rage. 'I'll see you in Switzerland, darling.' Her voice dripped with scorn and she swept past them with a violent kind of haste. 'And it will be my word against yours.' The door closed with a very loud bang as she slammed it behind her.

Isabella swallowed hard as she turned to face Brady. 'What on earth was that all about?' Her voice was very uneven as she forced herself to meet his dark gaze.

'Oh, I'm sorry, sweetheart.' He raked an impatient hand through his dark hair. 'She arrived a little while ago and tried to wheedle herself out of the mire with a lot of tears.'

'What mire?' Isabella frowned. 'Brady, what are you talking about?'

Brady sighed and led her by the hand back towards the settee. 'This isn't really what I want to be talking about at the moment,' he said with a gleam of humour. 'But before we get to more important things I suppose I had better explain.'

He sat down next to her on the settee and turned to look at her, his dark eyes intense on her face. 'You remember I told you that Gemma was the one who tried to steal Claude's notes on our new perfume?' he asked briskly.

She nodded. 'Of course I remember. I had thought you might bring it up at the board meeting.'

'No need. It's a Wolf-Chem problem more than Brook Mollinar's,' he replied briskly. 'Well, anyway, I had suspected Gemma wasn't quite the loyal secretary I had hoped for when I discovered her going through some papers in my office out of hours one night. She had a plausible excuse of sorts, but I kept a close eye on her after that. Then I decided to leave her a little test. I left my keys to Claude's safe on my office desk one night and, bingo, she took the bait.'

'You mean you deliberately set her up?' Isabella's eyes widened incredulously.

'It was the only way I could find out for sure what was going on,' Brady said with a grin. 'And I knew that Claude's files were incomplete as yet, so she could do no real damage.'

'So then what happened?' Isabella asked, trying to ignore how close Brady was sitting to her.

'Well, then I had to try and figure what my secretary would want with such confidential information...not an easy task. So I employed Noël to get some inside information, so to speak.'

'Noël! Noël was Gemma's boyfriend. He was in advertising.' Isabella was totally confused now.

Brady shook his head. 'No, you thought he was in advertising, as did Gemma. Really he was a private investigator.'

Isabella stared at his hard, handsome features. 'I can't believe this,' she said in a dazed voice.

'Well, I can assure you it is true. There was a lot of money at stake, Belle, and I had to do something. I knew that there was something behind Gemma's actions and I had to know what it was.'

'You could have just fired her straight away,' Isabella said with a wry lift of her shoulders.

'Oh, no, that would have been a mistake. Firstly I wouldn't have found out who was behind it all, and secondly it would have created a scandal without any positive results. I couldn't prove very much against Gemma; after all, she was dealing with my personal files all the time. I needed proof that she was going to pass it on to someone.'

'And Noël got you that proof?' she asked, impressed beyond words at Brady's efficient handling of the situation.

Brady nodded. 'Oh, yes, and the result was very interesting indeed. It would seem that our dear Roberta is the person behind it all.'

Isabella frowned. 'I don't understand, Brady.'

'Well…' He stroked a stray lock of her hair away from her face with a soothing hand. 'If you remember, Roberta once had a torch burning for me and I had to tell her in no uncertain terms that her feelings were not reciprocated. It seems that ever since then the woman has been extremely bitter towards me.'

'But what did she have to gain by access to our perfume?' Isabella asked, still puzzled.

'Well, recently there has been rather a struggle for power within the Wolf-Chem company, and much to Roberta's disgust I have taken control. I think her idea was to gain the information from our files and then make a public announcement that I had offered to trade Brook Mollinar secrets. Thus I would be discredited and she would be next in line for my position within Wolf-Chem.' He leaned back against the softness of the cushions, a weary expression on his face for a moment. 'It's all extremely tiresome. I shall be glad to be rid of Roberta from the company.'

'And will you?' Isabella asked breathlessly.

'Oh, yes, no doubt about it. Noël has some wonderful evidence against her, which is why she arrived on my doorstep this evening in tears.'

'And what about Gemma?'

He shrugged. 'Gemma was out to make some quick money. Let's not talk about this any more.' His eyes moved over her pale, delicate features in a searching way. 'So you liked my little gift?' he asked softly.

'The painting? Yes.' She nodded, her eyes suddenly bright. 'It's beautiful, Brady, thank you.'

'I thought so.' He paused. 'I had thought about hanging it in here…or maybe at the house in France.'

She frowned, not following him. 'Well, it was good of you to change your mind and give it to me.'

'Mmm,' he drawled softly. 'Well, I had thought we might share it.'

'How?' She stared into his dark eyes and watched him come closer with a feeling of breathlessness.

His lips touched hers gently. 'You know, Belle, I've loved you from the first moment I set eyes on you.' His voice was a husky murmur, barely audible, as his lips left hers.

She swallowed hard. She had to be imagining those words; it was probably wistful thinking.

His eyes searched her face; his finger traced the vulnerable curve of her lips. 'You were just seventeen and I couldn't believe the feelings you stirred up inside me,' he breathed softly.

She shook her head and suddenly her eyes filled with tears. 'Don't, Brady,' she whispered unsteadily. 'It's unfair of you to tease me like this.'

'I've never been more serious, my darling.' His lips curved in a gentle smile.

'I knew when your father asked me if you could stay at my house that summer after you turned eighteen that I would have a hard time trying to keep away from you. I tried to tell myself that you were really just a kid, that I owed it to your father and our friendship to treat you like just another young employee, but hell, Isabella.' He raked his hands through his dark hair. 'I knew all those things and yet I found it pure torture; I couldn't get enough of your smile, your gentle softness. I wanted you like crazy.'

Isabella stared at him in stunned disbelief, her heart beating so loudly that it seemed to fill her body with its heavy thud. 'But you sent me away,' she whispered unsteadily. 'You made it clear that you didn't want me.'

Brady shook his head. 'Belle, you were just eighteen, you were just starting out, you had so much in front of you, so much potential.' His voice sounded heavy for a moment. 'I couldn't take that away from you.'

'But you wouldn't have, Brady,' she burst out suddenly. 'I loved you, I wanted you. I thought my heart would break when you sent me away.'

His dark eyes filled with raw emotion at her passionate outburst. 'And I loved you, Belle. Don't you see? I had to send you away. It was the hardest decision I ever made. You had your university education to finish. If I hadn't made myself cut away from you I would have ruined your career, I would have ruined all the hard work you had already done.'

'I wouldn't have cared,' she burst out, her eyes bright and intense. 'I only cared about you.'

'You're speaking in the past tense, Belle.' His lips curved in a sad smile. 'So you see what you felt at eighteen isn't really what you feel at twenty-six. If I hadn't sent you away you could be sitting here now blaming me for ruining your opportunities, your life.'

Isabella shook her head. 'I might have regretted not going to university, but I would never have regretted loving you.' She swallowed hard. 'I loved you with everything inside me, Brady,' she whispered softly.

For a moment he said nothing, just stared at her with those incredibly dark eyes. 'And I loved you, Belle. It was because I loved you so much that I sent you away.'

Her heartbeat seemed to increase with the awful turmoil

inside her. He was speaking as if those feelings were in the past, as if they had died. 'Brady…' She shook her head, her vision blurring with tears. 'Please—'

He cut her short, his lips covering hers for a moment with a fierce, possessive kiss. 'You'll never know how hard it was to stay away from you,' he said as his lips left hers. 'I consoled myself with the thought that once you had left university and got yourself together I would come to you. Then you went to Paris…to Julien. When your father told me that you had plans to marry him, I nearly went demented. I told myself it was for the best, but inside it hurt.' His eyes glittered with a fierce anger for a moment. 'It hurt like hell to know that you had met someone immediately after leaving university when I had waited and hoped.'

Isabella bit down on the trembling softness of her lip, hope surging through her in a torrent of rich emotion. 'Julien was only ever a friend, Brady,' she told him gently. 'I guess I made more of the relationship in my letters home because I knew my father would tell you and I wanted you to think I was blissfully happy.' She shrugged helplessly. 'I still felt raw over you. I felt betrayed and very, very hurt when you sent me away…and I suppose in some foolish way I wanted you to know that someone else wanted me.'

'I think I nearly went out of my mind when I thought I'd lost you…' His deep voice trailed off. 'When you came back to London alone I couldn't believe it, hardly dared to hope I might have a second chance with you.'

Isabella caught her breath. 'Do…do you still feel the same? I mean…' Her face flushed a deep red as she forced herself to say the words that were burning inside her. 'I mean, do you still love me?'

'Oh, Belle, I love you more now than I've ever loved you,' he said in a deep velvet tone. 'After that night we spent together on the *Sequester* I even dared to think that you might feel the same way. Then I discovered that you suspected my involvement in the security leak.' His voice grew bitter. 'It was like a knife turning inside me. The fact that you hated me so much, that you felt nothing for me, that in actual fact you were still contemplating marrying Julien.'

'But I wasn't, Brady.' Tears trickled down the smooth paleness of her skin, her eyes blurring into misty blue pools. 'I love you, I've always loved you. Oh, I tried to hide from the fact, telling myself that you were all kinds of a monster, but that was my way of trying to keep my barriers up in case I got hurt again.'

He pulled her roughly into his arms and kissed her so passionately that she was breathless.

'Tell me again,' he demanded in a briskly authoritative tone. 'Tell me you love me, because, lord help me, I think I'm dreaming.'

She laughed through her tears. 'I...I love you, Brady... I always will.'

He kissed her and it was a while before another word was spoken. When he did lift his head he asked gruffly, 'And you will marry me at once?'

'Is that a proposal?' she asked, looking into his eyes.

'A direct order.'

Her lips twisted humorously. 'You know I don't like taking orders,' she murmured teasingly. 'But in this case...'

'Be quiet, woman.' He grinned and then kissed her masterfully. 'After all, I am going to let you make all the important decisions,' he said huskily.

'Such as?' she asked in disbelief.

'Well, for a start you can decide whether to hang our painting here or in our home in the South of France.'

Harlequin Books presents
the first title in Carly Phillips'
sizzling *Simply* trilogy.

"Carly Phillips's stories are sexy and packed
with fast-paced fun!"
—*New York Times* bestselling author Stella Cameron

Available in November 2003.

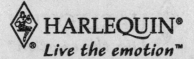

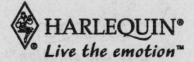

The world's bestselling romance series.

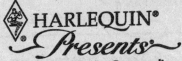

Seduction and Passion Guaranteed!

They're guaranteed to raise your pulse!

Meet the most eligible medical men of the world, in a new series of stories, by popular authors, that will make your heart race!

Whether they're saving lives or dealing with desire, our doctors have got bedside manners that send temperatures soaring....

Coming in Harlequin Presents in 2003:

THE DOCTOR'S SECRET CHILD by Catherine Spencer
#2311, on sale March

THE PASSION TREATMENT by Kim Lawrence
#2330, on sale June

THE DOCTOR'S RUNAWAY BRIDE by Sarah Morgan
#2366, on sale December

Pick up a Harlequin Presents® novel and you will enter a world of spine-tingling passion and provocative, tantalizing romance!

Available wherever Harlequin books are sold.

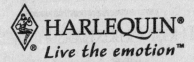

Visit us at www.eHarlequin.com

HPINTDOC

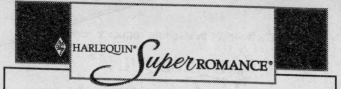

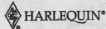

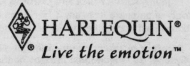

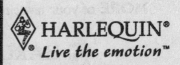

HARLEQUIN®
INTRIGUE®

Our unique brand of high-caliber romantic suspense just cannot be contained. And to meet our readers' demands, Harlequin Intrigue is expanding its publishing schedule to include **SIX** breathtaking titles every month!

Check out the new lineup in October!

MORE variety.
MORE pulse-pounding excitement.
MORE of your favorite authors and series.

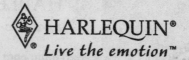

HARLEQUIN®
Live the emotion™

Visit us at www.tryIntrigue.com

HI4T06T